Friedrich

Friedrich

by Hans Peter Richter

Translated from the German by Edite Kroll

HOLT, RINEHART AND WINSTON
New York   Chicago   San Francisco

JU
F
R41

SBN: 03–085116–5 (Trade)
SBN: 03–085117–3 (HLE)

Library of Congress Catalog Card Number: 78–119098
Printed in the United States of America
First American Edition
Published in German by Walter-Verlag AG

Originally published in German
under the title *Damals war es Friedrich*

Contents

FRIEDRICH

Friedrich

Setting the Scene
(1925)

Someone had called him Polycarp, and he kept this name all the time he ruled over our front garden.

He wore green trousers, a red waistcoat, and a blue peaked cap. His left hand stuck in his trousers pocket, his right held a long pipe. He stood in the middle of the lawn and surveyed the garden like someone enjoying the end of a hard day's work.

Polycarp never moved from his spot. If the grass grew too high for him to see the dahlias by the fence, the landlord's wife would creep across the lawn on her knees and clip the blades to matchstick length with her garden shears.

We saw Herr Johann Resch, our landlord, only rarely. He never came outside except on holidays—*if* the weather was fine. Then he'd slowly stride to the center of the garden, his wife following with a chair. Snorting, he'd sit down next to Polycarp, his garden dwarf.

Herr Resch always stayed in his chair for exactly one hour, watching the passers-by in the street. Then he'd get up, circle around Polycarp, and puff his way back to the house. Until the next holiday he would watch Polycarp, the front garden, and the street from his window.

FRIEDRICH

Herr Resch wasn't just the owner of a house. He had begun as a salesman of bathing suits, but over the years he'd managed to get promoted to district manager. Now he let other salesmen do his work, while he conducted his business by telephone. At last Herr Resch could rule, and he let everyone feel it. His house was his seat of government—salesmen and tenants were his subordinates.

We lived on the second floor; that is, my parents lived there. My father was out of work, and was about to ask Herr Resch to exchange our apartment for a smaller one, when I was born.

By 1925 most Germans had run through their savings trying to survive the devaluation of the mark. There was very little prospect of finding work. Hardship and unemployment were on the rise throughout Germany.

So my parents were even more worried when I came into the world: I, too, wanted to eat and needed clothes. But I think they were pleased all the same.

Friedrich Schneider was born exactly one week later. The Schneiders lived in the same house, right above us. Herr Schneider was an official with the post office. My parents scarcely knew him. He always said a friendly good morning on his way to work, and an equally friendly good evening when he returned, but only rarely was there any real conversation.

My parents knew Frau Schneider, a small woman with dark hair, even less well. She would do her shopping or clean the stairs and immediately get back into her apartment. She smiled at everyone she met, but unlike her neighbors she never stopped to gossip. Our parents grew closer only after Friedrich and I were born.

Potato Pancakes
(1929)

Mother and I were still at breakfast when Frau Schneider rang our bell. She had been asked to go to city hall and didn't know how long she would be. She didn't want to take him with her either. Could he stay with us?

"Of course," my mother said. "Bring him down and the two boys can play together."

Half an hour later Friedrich was at the door. We knew each other, and had even quarreled. But although he had lived above us for four years, Friedrich had never been inside our apartment before.

Legs spread wide, I blocked the door to my room. My mother's pleas achieved nothing. I didn't budge. Defiantly I looked at Friedrich—I didn't want to share my toys with him.

Friedrich looked back. Then he squatted down with his back against our front door. He pulled a bit of twig from his pocket.

"My father was in the Black Forest," he said. "He brought me this whistle from there. It's a cuckoo whistle!"

FRIEDRICH

Friedrich lifted it to his mouth and blew "cuckoo." He put it down again and laughed.

My eyes must have grown very large. Each time Friedrich blew "cuckoo," I moved a step closer till I stood right in front of him.

Friedrich laughed again and pressed the cuckoo whistle into my hand.

At first I didn't understand. Speechless and stupid, I stared at him. Then I understood. I took Friedrich's sleeve, pulled him across the hall, and pushed him into my room and to my toys.

"You can play with them," I told him, saving only my bear. Bear at my side, I crouched in the corner beside my bed and blew "cuckoo," nothing but "cuckoo."

Friedrich started with my building blocks. He unpacked them and tried to build them into a tower. But the tower kept collapsing. At first Friedrich didn't mind. He even laughed. But then he got angry and scolded the wooden blocks. Finally, he toppled everything himself and looked for another toy. He found my truck. He piled the blocks into it and pulled the loaded truck across the room.

By this time, I'd had enough of cuckoo calls. My lips hurt and my jaw ached from the unaccustomed blowing. I put the whistle aside and got the train out of the toy cupboard.

Friedrich handed me the rails and I fitted them together. Then we set up the cars. I let Friedrich wind the engine. The train pulled off. If we wanted it to stop, we had to slide after it on our stomachs and adjust a lever in the caboose. But the train usually stopped by itself because the engine had run down. At first we played freight train, loading the cars with dried horse chestnuts. Then I showed Friedrich how to derail the train, and we played railroad disaster.

At last we grew tired of playing. Stretched out on the floor, we stared blankly at the lamp. Strewn all around us were building blocks, rails, chestnuts, railroad cars, old rags, and bits of paper. Only my bear still sat upright in his corner, surveying the mess.

Just then Mother came into the room. She asked us to help her make potato pancakes.

We only had potato pancakes on very special occasions. They were my father's favorite dish, and Mother always let us help her make them. Father usually ground the potatoes, and I chopped onions until my eyes watered.

Since Father wasn't home, I stuffed the peeled potatoes into the grinder and Friedrich turned the handle. Mother cut up the onions herself. Friedrich and I sprinkled flour over the batter and added a pinch of salt. We were very proud of our contribution!

Mother put the pan on the burner and poured oil into it. The oil began to splutter. It smelled delicious. Mother turned the pancakes. Ready! The edges were a crisp, dark brown, growing lighter toward the center, and changing into a grayish green.

Friedrich got the first potato pancake.

"Hot!" warned Mother.

Friedrich tossed the pancake from one hand to the other.
I grabbed it from him.
Friedrich got it back.
We wrestled.
Mother scolded.
The oil in the pan sputtered.
The pancake landed on the floor.

We came to an agreement. Friedrich bit into one side, I into the other. That way we ate all the potato pancakes.

A real feast! We leaned against the wall by the stove, tired and full.

"And you didn't leave a single one for Father," Mother said. "A pity!" She cleared away the pan, then looked us over. "You're a sight!" she decided. "Into the bathtub." What she said next was drowned by our bellows of joy.

Baths are grand, but they are much, much grander if two take them together. We slapped the water, shrieked, gurgled, shouted, splashed, and laughed.

Mother had to run from one end of the tub to the other, mopping up the water we kept spilling on the floor. Not until our landlord knocked at his ceiling did we calm down. Mother used this opportunity to scrub us clean. One soaping wasn't enough. Only after the third rinsing could you recognize us.

While I still splashed in the tub, Mother dried Friedrich, and said jokingly, "Well, Fritzchen! You look like a little Jew!"

Snow

(1929)

"Mother!" I said. "Look how beautifully it's snowing. I want to be out in it."

Mother answered from the kitchen. "I believe you. But work comes first, my boy, and then we'll go out in the snow."

The front garden was buried in snow. Only the tip of Polycarp's blue cap showed above the white blanket.

Although the flakes still fell calmly and evenly, Frau Resch came out into the front garden. With a shovel she scraped the snow from the flagstones and flung it to the side where the pruned rosebushes stood. By heaping the snow onto the border until a long hill stretched all the way to the garden gate, she cleared the whole path. Then she went back into her apartment.

"Mother!" I called. "Frau Resch has shoveled all the snow away!"

Mother laughed. "Don't you worry! More will fall, lots more!"

The house door banged shut. Friedrich ran to the gate and out. On the other side he jumped into the snow, both feet at once. Carefully he took one very large step, turned around, bent down, and looked at the prints his shoes had made. Then he straightened up. He threw back his head as far as it would go and opened his mouth to let the snow fall in. He even stuck out his tongue to catch snowflakes. He stood like that for quite a while and swallowed snow until he lost the taste for it. Then he looked at his footprints again. A new idea came to him. He began to stamp a trail in the snow. Because the snow whirled so beautifully, so like dust, Friedrich ran with both feet dragging. Clouds of snowflakes swirled around him.

"Mother," I asked, "are you going to be long? Friedrich's already playing in the snow."

Mother said, "You must learn to wait. Have a little patience."

Very quietly, Frau Schneider closed the front door. When she saw Friedrich in front of the next house, she crept up from behind. Before he could notice her, she had thrown snow over his head with both hands.

Friedrich shrieked and shook himself. He turned around. But when his mother only threw more snow at him, he ducked down, laughing. His fingers spread, he guarded his face. One leap! He stood before his mother. He hid his head under her coat and pushed tightly against her to escape from the flying snow.

Frau Schneider crouched down. Laughing, she hugged Friedrich against her and knocked the snow off his coat. Then she took hold of his shoulders and danced around with him in the snow.

"Mother," I implored, "Frau Schneider is now in the snow, too. Do please let's go down."

Mother sighed. "Don't pester me, boy," she said. "I'm working as fast as I can."

At the curb Frau Schneider looked left and right to see if the road was clear. Then she took a short run and slithered all the way across the road. She repeated this three or four times until one could see her path clearly. Then she took a few short steps, hopped onto the icy path, spread her arms wide, and glided safely across. One could see how much pleasure she got from doing this. When she had slid once again, she swayed, lost her balance; her feet rushed from under her—thump! She landed in the snow. Laughing, she stayed where she was and only scrambled to her feet when Friedrich tried to pull her up.

Friedrich, too, was allowed to slide. But he couldn't do it as well as his mother. After taking a run, he'd place his feet next to instead of behind each other, thrashing about in the air with his arms. But his mother always caught him before he fell.

"Mother," I begged. "The Schneiders are sliding now. Do hurry!"

Exasperated, Mother answered, "I'm going to finish the dishes before we go. The slide won't melt that fast."

Friedrich made some snowballs with clean snow. He squeezed them as hard as he could. He piled the finished snowballs up in front of our garden gate.

Frau Schneider also made snowballs. She collected her

pile on the sidewalk opposite. Because she worked faster than Friedrich, she helped him with his.

Then they began a snowball fight. Friedrich stood on our side of the street; because he couldn't throw as far as she, his mother positioned herself in the middle of the road. The snowballs flew back and forth. Friedrich made the first hit. While his mother was bending down to get more ammunition, his snowball burst on her back. But right after that there was a white speck on Friedrich's stomach.

Friedrich and his mother got red faces from bending down, jumping aside, throwing. They were gay and exuberant.

"Mother," I said sadly, "they're having a snowball fight. I'd so like to be there."

My mother consoled me. "I'll be ready in a second, my boy, and then we'll finally go."

Friedrich's mother searched for a spot where the snow was piled high. Again she formed a snowball, but this time she laid it back onto the snow. With her hand she carefully rolled it through the clean snow. The small ball quickly grew bigger. Every so often Frau Schneider stopped rolling to beat the snow firm.

At first, Friedrich stood beside his mother, watching curiously. Then he ran off. He, too, looked for a spot of unspoiled snow. Then, just like his mother, he began to roll a small snowball into a larger one.

Frau Schneider finished first. She had the bigger snowball. With all her strength she slammed it into the sidewalk in front of our house. To flatten the top she even sat on it. She then took Friedrich's ball and lifted it on top of hers. She filled in the gaps between the two balls with more snow, then patted everything nicely smooth and round.

"Mother," I burst out, "they're building a *snowman!*"

My mother calmed me down. "Yes, yes, I'm coming!" She brought my thick winter shoes and my coat. While she helped me put them on, she also looked out the window.

Frau Schneider and Friedrich were now rolling two snow pillars to make arms for the snowman. Friedrich handed the finished arms to his mother; Frau Schneider stuck them onto the snowman's chest. This didn't seem easy to do because the arms always threatened to break off again.

"You see, it's still snowing," my mother said. She knotted a woolen scarf around my neck; vigorously, she pulled the knitted cap down over my ears. For the first time I was allowed to wear the new mittens Mother had knitted for me. Mother looked me up and down. "So," she nodded, "now I'll get ready and then—into the snow!"

While Friedrich rolled a ball for the snowman's head, Frau Schneider rummaged in the trash can. She found several remnants of coal, some potato peel, and a broken beer bottle. Friedrich wheeled the large ball in front of her feet. She heaved it on top of the snowman. Into it she pressed the bottle neck for a nose, the coal bits for eyes, and the potato peel for ears—funny brown ears.

Mother stepped behind me, dressed to go out. "I'm ready. We can go." She looked out the window. "What a lovely snowman. All it needs is a hat." Apparently Frau Schneider wasn't satisfied with her snowman either. She examined it from all sides, shook her head, jiggled the keys out of her pocket, and came into the house.

Friedrich improved the snowman here and there, smoothed one side, and propped up the right arm. Then he looked at the front door and slowly sauntered toward it.

In the front garden he noticed the pile of snow beside the stone path. He climbed up, sank in and tramped through the high snow to the door, grinning.

At that moment, we heard a window flung open below us. Herr Resch bellowed, "Will you leave my roses in peace, you dirty Jewboy you!"

My mother stepped back. "Come," she said, "come away from the window."

Grandfather

(1930)

My grandfather on my mother's side worked for the railroad. He traveled a lot. Sometimes, when he passed through our town and could break his journey, he visited us. Each time, though, he announced his visit in advance by postcard.

As soon as Grandfather announced a visit, Mother feverishly began to put our apartment in order. She dusted where no dust was left, and spent the last of the household money to buy real coffee beans.

She scrubbed my hands with a vegetable brush until they hurt so much I couldn't touch anything with them. She parted my hair in the center and pasted it down with water so it wouldn't stand up in its usual mess.

At the given time I thus awaited Grandfather, standing behind our front door in my Sunday suit. The doorbell rang; I tore open the door. Bowing low, I said, "Good day, dear Grandfather. We are so glad to see you. *Herzlich willkommen."*

Without a word, Grandfather strode past me. Quickly, he marched through the apartment, inspecting every room with care. He didn't stop until he reached the living room.

We were allowed to shake hands then. He made me show him mine first. Both were clean. Then I had to turn around and lift up my feet one after the other. Grandfather wanted to see if the crosspiece between the sole and heel of each shoe had been polished with shoe cream. Since we knew about this whim, he didn't find anything to object to.

Afterwards Grandfather took his place—always the same one—at the living room table. He sat very straight. Father sat down opposite him; Mother remained standing behind Grandfather's chair so she wouldn't miss anything he asked for.

I crouched silently in the corner, red-scrubbed hands on cleanly washed knees. Whenever I moved, Mother looked at me; she laid a finger on her lips, reminding me to be silent.

Grandfather, as usual, talked at Father; he reproached him for not trying hard enough to find work. And Father listened with his head humbly lowered because he knew how the conversation would end. It always ran the same course. At the end, Grandfather said without fail: "If you had gone to the railroad as I did, you wouldn't have brought your family to such misery!"

Father nodded in resignation.

"But the boy," Grandfather always added, "the boy will go to the railroad. I will see to it myself. The boy shall have a secure future and be entitled to an old-age pension!"

Father agreed with Grandfather; he agreed with him in everything. Because Grandfather helped support us. As long as we had only Father's unemployment pay, Grandfather sent us money each month. This amount went into the household fund. Without it we'd have been hungry even more often. Suddenly, there was such a violent bump upstairs that our lamp shook.

"That was Friedrich!" I said.

Grandfather looked at me sternly. Then he asked Father, "Who is Friedrich?"

Father readily explained. "Above us lives a Jewish

family, the Schneiders. Their boy's name is Friedrich. The two are the same age; they are friends."

Grandfather cleared his throat. "A *Jewish* family?" he enquired.

"Yes," Father said, "nice people."

Grandfather said nothing for a while by pressing his lips hard together. Then he began: "I once had a superior who was a Jew. Cohn his name was. None of us liked him. He always smiled, even when he told you off. Friendly on the surface, he'd ask whoever it was made a mistake into his office. There he'd explain everything you'd done wrong, as if you were a schoolboy. And always with a special friendliness. One time—it was summer— I saw that he wore a square rag on his chest and back underneath his shirt, a prayer shawl with a fringe on it. He didn't even take his hat off in a room. No, I really don't like to remember Herr Cohn."

Neither Father nor Mother commented on Grandfather's story.

Grandfather looked at us. Then he said, "We are Christians. Bear in mind that the Jews crucified our Lord."

Here Father interjected, "But not the Schneiders!" Mother's face changed color.

Grandfather got up from the chair. He leaned on the table with his knuckles. So sharply it came out like a snarl, he ordered, "I do not wish the boy to associate with this Jew!" He sat down again as suddenly as he had stood up.

Father and Mother looked frightened. It was quiet, dreadfully quiet, in the living room.

The doorbell rang.

Mother hurried to the door.

Outside I heard Friedrich's voice: " . . . can he come upstairs please?"

Mother whispered: " . . . not possible . . . Grandfather's here."

She shut the door and returned to the living room. "Who was that?" Grandfather asked imperiously.

"A child from the neighborhood," Mother replied. "Would you like another cup of coffee?"

Friday Evening
(1930)

My mother did washing for other people. But no one was allowed to know because she was ashamed of it. Father was out looking for work, and I played with Friedrich in the Schneiders' apartment.

"What's that little tube you have over your doorpost?" I asked Friedrich.

Frau Schneider came into the room just then and answered for Friedrich. "That's our mezuzah," she said, "our home's blessing. It's to help us never to forget God and His commandments."

She took my hand and led me out of the room. On the way, she felt for the mezuzah with her right hand and kissed the fingers she had touched it with.

"Why don't you watch the street for a while," she begged me. "Friedrich still has to change and his father will be home any moment."

Before she went out the door she added more coal to the stove. She filled it all the way to the top and regulated it so that the coal would burn only weakly.

I stood alone in the living room. Mother wouldn't begin her weekly cleaning until tomorrow; Friedrich's mother had already finished hers. The table shone, there wasn't a speck of dust on any of the furniture, and the glass in the cabinets sparkled.

I was still admiring everything when Friedrich came back. He wore a white shirt and his best suit. Frau Schneider followed and pushed two chairs to the window for us; silently we looked out.

Outside it was already growing dark. Polycarp's peaked cap was difficult to distinguish from the grass. Lights were already on in a few apartments. One after the other the gas lamps in the street blazed up. Only a few people were about. It was very quiet.

But the Schneiders' apartment seemed unusually quiet. Frau Schneider spread a white cloth over the table, a cloth of such radiant white that it shone in the dim room. From the cupboard, she took two candlesticks with new candles in them. From the kitchen, she fetched two small home-made loaves of bread. These two loaves she placed on the table between the candlesticks and Herr Schneider's place.

FRIEDRICH

I had long stopped looking out the window. Instead I watched Frau Schneider at her preparations. Why so festive?

"What's going on?" I asked Friedrich in a whisper.

"Sabbath!" Friedrich replied in an equally low voice.

Only a thin, blood-red strip above the roof at the end of the block showed where the sun was going down. Everything was dipped in red.

Frau Schneider removed her kitchen apron. She took a large silver goblet from the cabinet and set it at Herr Schneider's place. Next to it she placed a prayer book. Then, turning to the wall bathed in red and murmuring something to herself, she lit both candles.

While Frau Schneider prayed, we heard Herr Schneider unlock the apartment door.

A moment later he entered the living room dressed in a dark suit and wearing a tiny embroidered cap.

Friedrich went to meet his father. Herr Schneider laid a hand on his head and said, "May God make thee as Ephraim and Manasseh. May the Lord bless thee and keep thee: May the Lord cause His countenance to shine upon thee, and be gracious unto thee. May the Lord lift up His countenance toward thee and give thee peace."

Then he opened the prayer book and read something to his wife in Hebrew.

Silent, her head bent low, Frau Schneider listened.

Still I stared wonderingly into the candlelight and did not know what to make of it all. Herr Schneider lifted the goblet from the table and filled it with wine. He held it with both hands and prayed.

Then we all drank a sip from it, first Herr Schneider, then Frau Schneider, then Friedrich, then me.

Herr Schneider left the room to wash his hands.

When he returned, he spoke over the homemade bread: "Blessed art Thou, O Lord our God, King of the Universe, Who brings forth bread from the earth."

He broke one loaf and handed each of us a piece. We ate silently.

In our apartment someone was running water from the tap. "Your mother's home," Frau Schneider said in a low voice. "If you like, you could take her a few pears. They'll only get soft otherwise. The basket's in the hall."

I said good-bye and thank you and, with the pears, went downstairs to my mother.

Before falling asleep, I could still hear the Schneiders singing together, softly and sadly.

School Begins
(1931)

Friedrich and I were allowed to sit on the same bench. Our teacher told us a story. Then we all sang "Little Hans" and our first school day was over.

Our parents waited for us outside the school gate. Father was out of work in any case, and Herr Schneider had taken the day off.

FRIEDRICH

Like all German children after their first day at school, Friedrich and I each received a large, cone-shaped paper bag from our parents. Friedrich's was red, mine blue. My blue bag was a little smaller than Friedrich's red one.

Friedrich opened his right away. He offered me one of his pieces of candy and broke a bar of chocolate so that everyone could have some.

I was about to undo the bow on my paper bag when Mother shook her head. She took me aside and told me I should wait until we got home. I couldn't understand why, but I obeyed.

At the next street corner, Herr Schneider asked loudly: "And where to now?" Smiling, he looked at us all.

Everyone regarded Herr Schneider expectantly, only Father shot a frightened glance at Mother.

Friedrich answered the question. Jubilantly he shouted, "To the amusement park!"

Again Father looked at Mother; this time his eyes were anxious. Mother told Herr Schneider, "What a pity we can't come with you. I have so much to do at home, and I haven't even prepared lunch yet."

"But Mother," I implored her, "I'd so much like to go to the amusement park."

Father stroked my head. "We can't, my boy. Think of Mother."

But Herr Schneider seized my mother's arm, and Frau Schneider linked her arm with Father's. "No excuses valid today!" Herr Schneider explained. "On the first day of school we are going to the amusement park."

Father and Mother looked very downcast. But they went.

Friedrich pushed three pieces of chocolate into my mouth at once, then we raced ahead of our parents, arm in arm, paper bags in our hands.

At the amusement park, the fathers took our hands. My father edged unobtrusively toward Mother. "You must lend me five marks," I heard him whisper in her ear.

"But I don't have any money with me," Mother whispered back. "Just two marks of my household money."

Father groaned. Then he said, "Give me the two marks! I have another seventy pfennigs in my pocket."

Mother burrowed in her pocketbook. Supposedly looking for her handkerchief, she furtively pushed the two marks into Father's hand.

Father looked unhappy. I was already sorry I had asked to go to the amusement park. The Schneiders marched ahead; we followed listlessly.

We stopped at the merry-go-round. We watched it spin. Suddenly Friedrich pushed a ticket into my hand. When the carousel stopped, we handed the paper bags to our mothers and climbed onto the horses. Mine was called Bella; the saddle blanket on Friedrich's was inscribed "Fox." It was wonderful to ride round and round again; we waved, and bounced, and shouted, and urged our horses on, until the merry-go-round stopped.

Herr Schneider bought us new tickets so we could ride a second time.

When the carousel again came to a stop, Herr Schneider and his wife, and Father and Mother as well, clambered up. They mounted the horses behind us and we all rode together.

Afterward Frau Schneider bought each of us an enormous stick of cotton candy.

While we ate the cotton candy, Father, with a desperate face, kept counting his money in front of each stand we passed. He was trying to see if he had enough to buy something for everyone.

"What shall I do?" he asked in a whisper.

Mother shrugged her shoulders hopelessly.

Herr Schneider treated everyone to a long knockwurst with mustard and a roll.

In his distress Father could hardly get it down.

I knew Mother loved knockwursts at fairs, but I could see she didn't enjoy this one because she was worrying.

Suddenly Father disappeared. He came back carrying six sticks of licorice.

Frau Schneider was so delighted she seemed never to have had anything so beautiful. Soon everyone was sucking a licorice stick.

Father heaved a sigh of relief.

We children were allowed to go on the fire engine ride. Then we watched our parents—Herr Schneider with my mother, Father with Frau Schneider—on the swing boats.

Friedrich yawned; I, too, was tired.

"Enough for today!" said Herr Schneider. "Come on! Home!"

School Begins

At the far end of the amusement park, Father finally hit the right booth.

REMEMBRANCE PHOTOS
1 POSTCARD 1 MARK
2 POSTCARDS 1 MARK 50 PFENNIGS

the sign read. At once, Father made for the owner. "Take a picture of us," he said. "We'll take two postcards."

The owner of the booth bowed. "Step closer, ladies and gentlemen," he murmured. "Step closer please!"

Inside, a mountain scene had been painted on the back wall. Before it stood a piebald wooden horse. "Please have a seat," said the man.

"Where?" asked Father.

"On the horse," said the man.

"But two at most will fit on that," Father said.

"Just a moment!" said the man. He gripped the horse's tail as if he wanted to tear it out. He put the tail over his shoulder and pulled hard.

Slowly the wooden horse stretched, grew longer and longer, so long that ten grownups would have found room on it comfortably.

When Herr Schneider saw the stretched-out horse he couldn't stop laughing. I had never seen him laugh so hard. His wife had to hold on to him so he wouldn't fall over.

My father proudly mounted the endless horse. The owner of the booth brought a foot bench and helped the women up. Last of all he hoisted up the children.

(23)

When Herr Schneider climbed on, he nearly fell off the other side, he still shook so with laughter.

Finally we all were squatting, one behind the other, on the wooden horse. Our mothers held us tightly, otherwise we would surely have slid off from sheer fatigue. Only Father propped a hand on his hip. Proudly he rode in the middle, head held high. And Herr Schneider laughed; he laughed so hard at the accordion horse that he infected all of us. Even Father smiled, if only a little.

The owner disappeared behind the black cloth of his camera, only his hands poked out from it. He gave instructions no one understood. At last, he changed the ground glass screen for the photographic plate, stood beside the camera, growled "Attention!" and pressed down the red rubber ball.

Holding ourselves motionless, we stifled our laughter and stared into the camera until the man said, "Thank you." He disappeared into the darkroom with the plate, and we hopped down from the horse.

At once Herr Schneider began to pull the horse's tail. And behold! It stretched still further. Herr Schneider lengthened the horse till it reached the side wall of the booth. When we regarded it in all its length against the mountain scene, even Father had to laugh out loud.

Then the booth owner brought us the two postcards and Father generously paid him from his jacket pocket. With a bow he handed one postcard to Frau Schneider.

I sat in front. The wooden horse carried my paper bag between its ears. Behind me rode Mother. She pulled a face ,as if she had a frog in her mouth that mustn't hop out. Father lorded it in the center. (Everyone who saw the picture had to assume that the horse belonged to him.) Friedrich held on to Father's jacket. His paper bag towered above all the mountaintops and seemed to help support the clouds. Little Frau Schneider had grabbed hold of Friedrich's collar. She really looked very dear. Herr Schneider embraced her laughingly from behind.

On the way home everyone was still happy, thinking about the "remembrance" pictures. Only Father felt ashamed because he had taken himself so seriously on the wooden horse.

When we reached home, I stumbled exhaustedly into the hall. I quickly threw the new satchel into the corner and untied the bow on my paper bag. It contained nothing but a bag of sugared rusks and lots and lots of crumpled paper.

Mother stroked my hair. "But you know, my boy," she said, "that we are poor."

Father washed his hands and asked, "What's for lunch today?"

Mother sighed. "Nothing!" she replied. "We spent the lunch money at the amusement park."

The Way to School
(1933)

It was Saturday, April 1, 1933. We were coming out of school. Friedrich said, "My mother dragged me to the doctor yesterday afternoon, you know. She wanted him to wash out my ears. He didn't, though."

"Why not?" I asked.

Friedrich laughed. "He said it wasn't necessary yet. To start with I'm to take this restorative he prescribed. It's quite sweet and not bad. He told me three spoonfuls a day would make me so strong I could stand having the stuff taken out of my ears."

I looked curiously at Friedrich. "And?"

Friedrich shrugged. "I took five because it tasted so good."

He still hadn't given me the right answer, so I asked again, "What about your ears?"

Friedrich pushed out his lower lip. Then he said, "Mother cleaned my ears last night."

I still wasn't satisfied. "Did you scream?"

Eyes cast down, Friedrich admitted, "Only a little."

Silently we walked side by side. It was a Saturday like any other Saturday—the traffic moved smoothly, women were doing their weekend marketing, and we had almost no homework.

"Which doctor do you go to?" I asked Friedrich.

"We'll be going by his house any minute now," he answered, pointing to an apartment house.

"That's his sign," he said.

A doctor's white sign hung beside the front door. In flourishing black script it read:

> DR. JAKOB ASKENASE
> SPECIALIST FOR CHILDREN'S AILMENTS
> LICENSED TO ALL INSURANCE COMPANIES
> OFFICE HOURS: 9 AM–12 NOON AND 3 PM–7 PM
> DAILY EXCEPT SATURDAY.

Across it, someone had scrawled the word "Jew" in red paint.

Friedrich shook his head. "Who could have done that?" He touched the paint with his finger. "It's still wet."

Friedrich looked around. "Come on," he said, stepping through the outside door and pressing a bell beside the name "Dr. Askenase."

We waited.

"He has no office hours today," I pointed out. "Maybe he isn't in."

We were just going to leave when the buzzer sounded. Friedrich threw his back against the inner door until it opened. We climbed just a few steps and stood outside the door with the doctor's sign.

A middle-aged man in a dark suit appeared. A yarmulke was on his head. When he saw Friedrich, he smiled and asked, "Well, Friedrich, any flowers growing out of your ears yet?"

Friedrich blushed, and in a faint voice he replied, "No, my mother cleaned them yesterday."

The doctor nodded. "There you are," he said. "I knew that good medicine would make you sensible. Or don't you like it?"

"Oh yes," Friedrich quickly agreed, licking his lips. Then he added, "This is my friend. You'll have to prescribe some for him one day too."

Dr. Askenase shook my hand. "In that case, you and your mother will have to come and see me," he said. He went on, "But you didn't come about that, did you? Friedrich knows I don't see patients on Saturday, don't you?"

Friedrich seemed confused. "We wanted to let you know . . . " he began.

". . . that someone scrawled the word 'Jew' all over your sign downstairs," I finished for him.

"I know!" said the doctor. "I read it. Don't worry, I'll remove it tomorrow." Dr. Askenase had turned serious. He lightly touched our hair and shook hands again. "Thank you for coming. And now get home quickly." He was no longer smiling as he closed the door behind us.

When we came out of his house, we saw people had gathered at the next corner.

"An accident!" guessed Friedrich.

We unbuckled the satchels on our backs and put them under our arms.

I bounded ahead. At the corner was a small stationery shop. To get into it you had to go down a few steps. Besides ink, drawing pads, and colored paper, it also sold candy: chocolate bars at five pfennigs each or licorice at two pfennigs a stick. The shop belonged to a little old man with a pointed beard. We bought our notebooks in his shop. The old man was always kind and friendly. Often he took a pfennig off the price and gave us some candy as well.

Sometimes we had made fun of the old man and his goat's voice, bleating loudly as we came down his stairs. But he never took this amiss. Indeed, it sometimes occurred to us that he would bleat extra loud for our sakes.

Outside his shop a crowd had collected. The people stood pressed so closely together that one couldn't see what was going on. A few were laughing and jeering, others looked serious.

We shoved our way to the front of the throng to see better. No one hindered us; a young woman even gave us a push forward.

Beneath the sign ABRAHAM ROSENTHAL, STATIONERY a man in gray breeches straddled the entrance to the shop. His puttees were untidily wound around his calves. He wore an armband with a swastika on the left sleeve of his yellow shirt.

In his right hand he held a broomstick, an ordinary

(29)

broomstick, and fastened to it was a cardboard sign that read, in clumsy letters:

DON'T BUY FROM JEWS.

On old woman carrying a worn shopping bag walked up to the sign. From her coat pocket she pulled a pair of glasses that were missing one ear piece. Holding them close to her eyes, she tried to read the sign.

The sign carrier pretended not to notice the old woman, staring right over her at the crowd.

The woman put her glasses back in her pocket. Searchingly she pattered back and forth in front of the man with the armband; finally, she stopped and said quietly: "Kindly let me pass!"

Without moving and without looking at the woman, the picketer recited in a monotone: "DON'T BUY FROM JEWS!"

"But I want to!" the old woman insisted; and when the man didn't budge, she squeezed between him and the wall and flitted down the stairs and into the shop.

The bystanders grinned. In the back rows, some even laughed out loud.

The man with the sign didn't move a muscle; only his left hand, thumb stuck behind the buckle of his belt, clenched into a fist.

Shortly afterward the old woman pulled herself up the stairs. A roll of blue wrapping paper for schoolbook covers peaked out of her bag. Smiling, the woman—leading with her shoulder—pushed herself past the man. With a nod, she told him, "Thank you very much, young man." Holding herself very straight, she walked past the crowd, carrying the shopping bag in such a way that everyone could see the wrapping paper she had bought. Nearsightedly, she smiled at them all and walked away.

Abraham Rosenthal stepped into the doorway of his basement shop. His face serious, he peered at the people outside his shop.

Politely Friedrich greeted Herr Rosenthal so pointedly that no one could fail to notice.

I merely nodded to him.

The little man with the pointed beard answered with a silent bow. Through clenched teeth the sign bearer snarled at us: "Get away from here, go on!"

Friedrich looked him up and down and said, "We can stand here as long as you can!"

The man pushed out his lower jaw; taking a deep breath he asked in a threatening voice: "Want to be fresh, brat?"

A few people walked away, the rest drew back a step. All of a sudden it was utterly quiet; no one talked, no one laughed.

We stood alone. The man breathed hard. The cardboard sign shook.

I saw a hand settling on Friedrich's shoulder at the same time that I felt a touch on mine.

We both turned around.

Behind us stood Friedrich's father. He said: "Come!"

Then he took us home.

The Jungvolk
(1933)

I ran down the stairs. At the front door, I pressed the Schneiders' bell: three times short, once long, that was our signal. Then I sauntered through the front garden past Polycarp and walked to the corner.

Friedrich arrived almost at once. "Thanks a lot," he said breathlessly. "Thanks so much for fetching me."

Side by side, we walked in the direction of the park. We were early and didn't have to hurry.

"I'm so glad, you know!" Friedrich began afresh. "But you mustn't tell my father. He doesn't like my going there. You know, I saw you all marching through town with your flag and singing. I think that's really great. I'd love to take part, but Father won't let me join the *Jungvolk*. Still, maybe he'll change his mind after a while."

We ambled through the park. Through the trees, we could make out the brown brick buildings of the old fortress.

"What's on for today?" asked Friedrich. "More war games?"

I shook my head. "Wednesdays are club nights. We can

bring strangers only on Wednesdays. But you'd better
not mention right away that you're a Jew."

Friedrich put his arm around my shoulder and whispered to himself, "Oh, I'm so pleased!"

"Our squad leader's a great fellow," I told him. "He's
been a member for ages. You can see his neckerchief
pinned to the wall of the clubhouse; it has a cut right
through the middle. He wore it during a raid. A communist tried to stab him, but his knife only cut the cloth
and he wasn't harmed."

Friedrich fished around in his trouser pocket. "I almost
forgot about this!" he shouted, pulling out a black, three-
cornered scarf. "I swiped it from Mother's first aid box,"
he said, smiling.

We stopped at the next park bench. I showed Friedrich
how to roll his scarf according to regulations, then I
placed it underneath his white shirt collar so that only a
corner hung out in back. I was just about to tie a knot
in front when Friedrich pulled a ring from his trouser
pocket. It was made of brown leather and had a swastika
stamped in it. Not even our squad leader owned such a
grand ring.

Friedrich proudly slid the ring over the rolled ends
of the triangular scarf all the way to his neck. When he
saw how I envied him his ring he was still more delighted.
He pushed out his chest, fell into step with me, and
together we marched through the old fortress gate to
the parade grounds.

The others were already in the courtyard; they didn't

(33)

pay any attention to us. Most of them wore short pants and any old striped or checked shirt; only a few owned the regulation brown shirt. Strictly speaking, no one was properly dressed. The only thing everyone had in common was the triangular neckerchief with the corner showing below the shirt collar in back.

With shining eyes Friedrich leaned against the wall beside me. "I'm so glad I can be here!" he said, touching his neckerchief ring.

My platoon leader arrived at last. He was about fifteen and wore the regulation uniform we all longed for.

I reported that I had brought a new boy. "In order!" he said. "But I don't have time now. We'll take care of it later!" Then he ordered us all to fall in line. We fell in line.

I pushed Friedrich into the back row next to me.

"Right turn! Close it up! Single file!"

There was some confusion because Friedrich didn't quite know how to march in single file. He got a few jabs in his ribs before he stamped behind me up the narrow, winding stairs.

Our club house was a windowless room in the old fortress. A strong bulb dangled from the ceiling by two wires. Entering, one's eyes met the picture of Adolf Hitler on the wall facing the door. Underneath the picture our squad leader's famous scarf was stretched to full width. The many fingers that had reverently passed over the fabled cut had widened it to a hole so large you could stick your head through it.

The Jungvolk

On the right wall hung two crossed poles, their black pennants fastened with pins to the wall. The white embroidered victory rune, ⚡, sign of the *Jungvolk,* looked resplendent in the center of the black pennant.

On the wall beside the door, a platoon leader had tried his hand at maxims in watercolor. "Be more than you seem!" was one, and a second read: "Fight for your Life!"

Friedrich shivered with excitement as he sat down beside me on the wooden bench. "Great!" he whispered. "I'm so glad I'll be joining the *Jungvolk* and become a *Pimpf.*"

We had hardly sat down when my platoon leader bellowed: "Attention!" Everyone jumped up and stood facing Hitler's picture. The platoon leader spoke to our squad leader.

With heavy tread our squad leader stepped beneath the picture. He lifted his hand. *"Sieg Heil, boys!"*

"Sieg Heil, Fähnleinführer!" we replied.

Friedrich shouted it with such enthusiasm his voice broke and tears came into his eyes.

"Sit down!" ordered the squad leader, and above the din of dropping onto the benches, he began: "Boys, I brought someone special to our club evening tonight. He is Special Delegate Gelko from the District Office of our party. He wants to talk to you about something very important."

Only then did I notice the hunchback. He was so short he didn't stand out among the boys. He was covered from

(35)

head to toe in brown; he even wore brown boots. The visor of his cap—also brown—hid his face.

He walked to the front. But he couldn't see the whole room. In the end, the platoon commander brought an empty orange crate. The hunchback climbed onto it and began his speech.

"Pimpfe of our *Führer!"* The voice was unpleasantly shrill. "I have been delegated to talk to you today about the Jews. You all know Jews. But you all know too little about them. This will be different an hour from now. You will then know what a danger Jews represent for us and our nation."

Friedrich sat bent slightly forward beside me on the bench. His eyes hung on the speaker. His mouth slightly open, he devoured every word.

The hunchback seemed to feel this and soon it looked as if he were addressing his speech to Friedrich alone. His words were effective. He was able to paint everything in such colors that we believed it was actually happening before our eyes. What he now told us made even those with colds forget to cough.

"With a large knife," he said, "a knife as long as my arm, the Jew priest steps beside the poor cow. Very slowly, he raises the knife. The beast feels the threat of death; it bellows, tries to wrench free. But the Jew knows no mercy. Quick as a flash he drives the wide knife into the animal's neck. Blood spurts; it befouls everything. The animal is in a frenzy, its eyes fixed, staring in horror. But the Jew knows no pity; he doesn't shorten its suffering; he wallows in the pain of the bleeding animal; he wants that blood. And he stands by and watches the animal slowly bleeding to its pitiful death. It's called kosher butchering!—The God of the Jews demands it!"

Friedrich bent so far forward I was afraid he'd topple off the bench. His face was pale, his breathing labored; his hands clutched his knees.

The hunchback told of murdered Christian children, of Jewish crimes, of wars.

Just listening made me shudder.

Finally the speaker ended: "One sentence, one sentence only I want to hammer into your brains; I will repeat it until it comes out of your ears, and repeat it: The Jews are our affliction! And again: The Jews are our affliction. And another time: *The Jews are our affliction!*"

Sweating and exhausted, the little special delegate stood on his orange box. It was completely quiet in the room.

Then the hunchback pointed to Friedrich. "What is the sentence?" he asked him.

Friedrich didn't move.

"What is the sentence?" the speaker asked more sharply.

Friedrich sat stiffly and hunched forward beside me on the bench.

"What is the sentence?" The voice of the special delegate cracked. He hopped off the box and walked toward Friedrich with pointed finger.

Friedrich swallowed.

The hunchback stood before him. His eyes stabbed at Friedrich. He grabbed his scarf and slowly pushed the ring upwards.

"What is the sentence?" he barked.

In a faint voice Friedrich said, "The Jews are our affliction."

The hunchback hauled Friedrich up from the bench in one movement. "Stand up when I talk to you!" he screamed in his face. "And reply loudly if you please!"

Friedrich stood up straight. He was still pale. In a clear voice he proclaimed: "The Jews are our affliction."

There wasn't a sound. Friedrich turned around. The ring was in the hunchback's hand.

Friedrich left the club unhindered. I stayed where I was.

The Ball
(1933)

We ran along the street. Friedrich kept close to the houses; I stayed on the curb. I threw the little rubber ball I'd been given in the shoe store. It hit the center of the sidewalk and bounced high. Friedrich caught it and threw it back to me.

"My father will be home any moment!" he called to me. "I must get back soon. We're going shopping today. Maybe someone'll give me a ball, too!"

I nodded and jumped over a manhole. I waited until a pedestrian had gone by, then hurled the ball back to Friedrich.

(38)

The Ball

Friedrich hadn't been watching.

There was a crash.

The ball rolled harmlessly back to me.

Friedrich stared openmouthed at the smashed shop window. I bent to pick up the ball, not yet believing what had happened.

Suddenly the woman stood before us. She grabbed Friedrich's arm and began to screech.

Doors and windows opened. A crowd gathered.

"Thieves! Burglars!" the woman shouted.

Her husband stood by the shop door, hands in his pockets, smoking a pipe.

"This good-for-nothing Jewboy here broke my shop window," she told everyone who cared to listen. "He wants to rob me." She turned to Friedrich. "But you didn't quite make it this time, did you. Because I'm always watching. I know you, you won't get away from me. You pack of Jews, they should get rid of you. First you ruin our business with your department stores, then you rob us on top of it! Just you wait, Hitler will show you yet!" And she shook Friedrich violently.

"But he didn't do it!" I yelled. "*I* threw the ball, *I* broke your window. We didn't want to steal!"

The woman looked at me, eyes large and stupid. Her mouth dropped open.

Her husband had swept the broken glass into the gutter. He collected the rolls of thread, the stars of black and white yarn, the balls of colorful embroidery yarn from the display case and carried them into the shop.

FRIEDRICH

The woman's eyes grew very small. "How dare you interfere? What are you doing here anyway? Away with you! You don't think you have to protect this rotten Jewboy because you're living in the same house, do you? Go on, beat it!"

"But I threw the ball!" I said again.

The woman lunged at me, without letting go of Friedrich. Friedrich cried. He wiped his tears on his sleeve, smearing his whole face.

Someone had called the police.

Out of breath and sweating, a policeman arrived on a bicycle. He asked the woman to tell him what had happened.

Again she told the story of the attempted burglary.

I tugged at his sleeve. "Officer," I said, "he didn't do it. I broke the pane with my ball."

The woman looked at me threateningly. "Don't you believe him, Officer!" she said. "He only wants to protect the Jewboy here. Don't you believe him. He thinks the Jew's his friend just because they live in the same house."

The policeman bent down to me. "You don't understand this yet, you're too young still," he explained. "You may think you're doing him a favor by standing up for him. But you know he's a Jew. Believe me, we grownups have had plenty of experiences with Jews. You can't trust them; they're sneaky and they cheat. This woman was the only one who saw what happened, so . . . "

"But she didn't see it!" I interrupted him. "Only I was there, and I did it!"

The Ball

The policeman frowned. "You wouldn't try to call this woman a liar." I wanted to explain, but he didn't let me.

He took Friedrich's wrist from the woman and led him toward our house, followed by the woman and a long line of curious onlookers.

I joined the line.

Halfway there we ran into Herr Schneider.

Sobbing, Friedrich shouted, "Father!"

Astonished, Herr Schneider surveyed the procession. He came closer, said hello, and looked from one person to another, obviously puzzled.

"Your son—" said the policeman.

But the woman didn't give him a chance to go on. In one burst she repeated her tales. The only part she left out this time was her insinuation about Jews.

Herr Schneider listened patiently. When she had finished, he took Friedrich's chin in his hand and lifted his head so he could look into his eyes.

"Friedrich," he asked seriously, "did you break the shop window intentionally?"

Friedrich shook his head, still sobbing.

"I did it, Herr Schneider. I threw the ball, but I didn't do it on purpose!" And I showed him my small rubber ball.

Friedrich nodded.

Herr Schneider took a deep breath. "If you can swear on oath that what you just told me is the truth," he told the woman, "go ahead and register a formal complaint. You know me, and you know where I live!"

(41)

The woman did not reply.

Herr Schneider pulled out his purse. "Kindly release my son, Officer!" he said sharply. "I will pay for the damage at once."

Conversation on the Stairs
(1933)

Herr Schneider and Friedrich were coming down the stairs. I could see them through a crack in the door.

Herr Resch was dragging his weight up the steps by holding on to the banister. On the landing outside our door he stopped to catch his breath.

There they all met.

Herr Schneider said hello and was about to go on.

Herr Resch did not return the greeting. He blocked Herr Schneider's way. He breathed heavily; his face turned red. Finally he burst out: "I wanted to talk to you."

Herr Schneider said, "Certainly," and made a small bow to Herr Resch. He took the keys from his pocket. "May I ask you to step into my apartment, Herr Resch. I believe it is easier to talk in the living room than on the stairs." With a gesture of his hand he offered Herr Resch precedence.

Herr Resch refused. "Never again will I set foot in your

apartment," he said. "I am just as glad I met you here. What there is to discuss can be settled here."

Herr Schneider cleared his throat, made another slight bow, and said, "Just as you wish, Herr Resch!"

Herr Resch took his time. He shuffled as far as our door and pressed the bell.

Father opened the door. I peered out from behind him.

"Would you please listen in," Herr Resch asked my father. "I need you as a witness."

Father stayed in the doorway without saying a word. Puzzled, he looked from Herr Resch to Herr Schneider, and back.

Herr Schneider looked at my father and shrugged.

Friedrich clung anxiously to the banister.

Herr Resch took a deep breath; he coughed, once more breathed deeply. "I hereby give you notice for the first!" he finally spluttered.

No one said a word. Only Herr Resch's excited, gasping breaths were audible. Father's and Herr Schneider's eyes locked together; Herr Resch lowered his eyes to the floor. Friedrich examined the stair lights, and I understood nothing.

"I beg your pardon?" said Herr Schneider.

"You move out on the first!" declared Herr Resch.

Herr Schneider smiled as he said, "You can't be serious, Herr Resch!"

"But you can't do that, Herr Resch," my father interrupted. "Herr Schneider has his rights as a tenant."

Herr Resch shot a mean glance at my father. "I didn't

(43)

ask you to support this gentleman!" he snapped. "You are supposed to be a witness, nothing else!"

My father cleared his throat. "You cannot order me to be quiet, Herr Resch. Do not count on me as a witness!" He pushed me back and slammed the door.

But we stayed behind it to listen.

Politely, Herr Schneider took the conversation up again. "It really isn't done to give me such short and unexpected notice, Herr Resch."

Pretending to cough, Herr Resch replied: "You will see, it can be done."

Herr Schneider inquired, "And may I ask why you are giving me notice?"

So loud that it reverberated through the whole house, Herr Resch's shout was: "Because you are a Jew!" We heard him stamp down the stairs.

Herr Schneider

(1933)

We sat at the curb outside our house.

Friedrich was explaining the math problems.

I hadn't paid any attention in class, and I didn't pay attention to Friedrich either. With my shoe I pushed a rock to and fro on the pavement.

Friedrich worked out sums with such concentration that he didn't notice I wasn't listening. But he jumped when I kicked the rock hard. He followed it with his eyes.

I tried to make out what fascinated him so.

There wasn't a thing to be seen. The street was empty. Far off a single man walked. Slowly he came closer.

"Is that my father?" Friedrich asked softly.

I looked once more at the man in the distance. "No," I said, "your father walks faster. And anyway, it's too early; he can't have finished work yet."

Friedrich didn't answer. His eyes followed every movement of the approaching man.

The man carried a briefcase by the handle. His head hung on his chest, a hat shaded his face. The man dragged his feet. Sometimes he stopped, hesitated. Then he turned toward a garden gate. Half a step away from it, he wavered and veered toward the street again.

"He is drunk!" I said.

"It's my father after all!" Friedrich cried out, leaping up and running toward the swaying man.

I sat on, not trusting Friedrich's eyes. I saw how Friedrich stopped short just before he reached the man. Then he took his arm. The man didn't look up once. Friedrich led the way. As the two came closer, I recognized Herr Schneider.

Blocking my view of his father, Friedrich pulled him across the sidewalk by the sleeve. Turning his back, he led his father past me into our front garden.

Herr Schneider never missed saying hello. But this time

he kept his eyes lowered. Tears ran down his face. He did not wipe off the tears; they rolled onto his jacket and left a damp trail.

Herr Schneider wept! I had never seen a man cry before.

Friedrich and his father disappeared into the house.

I still stood at the curb. Only when I imagined Friedrich and his father safely inside their apartment did I go upstairs.

I told Mother about Herr Schneider weeping.

Mother said, "We will be very quiet. I am sure Herr Schneider has gone through something dreadful. We do not want to disturb him."

I went to the kitchen and tried to read. But actually I thought about Herr Schneider.

Toward evening Frau Schneider came down. She was paler than usual and her hair was untidy. Anxiously, she looked around our kitchen.

Mother was working at the stove. "What is upsetting your husband, Frau Schneider?" Mother asked quietly, not looking at her. "Has he worries?"

Frau Schneider shook her head. Suddenly she collapsed onto one of our kitchen chairs. She threw her arms on the table, laid her face in them and cried, loudly and violently. The sobs shook her body and they didn't stop. Again and again she stammered, "I am afraid! I am so afraid!" One could barely make out the words.

My mother had turned in alarm when Frau Schneider collapsed on our kitchen table. Now she asked no questions and said nothing further. From the farthest corner of the kitchen cupboard she took the strictly guarded can of real coffee beans. She ground the beans and after rinsing it with hot water put six heaped teaspoons into the little coffee pot, which held only three cups.

Frau Schneider still sobbed. Her tears made a small puddle on the wax tablecloth.

Mother brewed up the coffee by pouring boiling water on the ground beans. While the grounds settled to the bottom of the pot, she fetched a bottle of brandy. This brandy—at Father's request—was only used for serious illnesses. Mother opened the bottle. She poured the coffee and added a large portion of brandy.

Frau Schneider noticed none of this. In between her sobs we heard more unintelligible scraps of words.

My mother took a kitchen chair and sat down close to Frau Schneider. She lifted her head and dabbed her face. Then she gently forced the strong hot coffee laced with brandy down her throat in spoonfuls.

It took a long time for Frau Schneider to calm down. Finally she got hold of herself. With a damp cloth, which Mother handed her, she cooled her tear-reddened eyes. "Please forgive me," she whispered. "I'm so upset."

Mother shook her head. She stroked Frau Schneider's hair. "Why don't you tell me all about it, it will ease your burden."

Frau Schneider nodded. Again and again, tears came to her eyes. After a while she said so softly one could hardly catch the words, "My husband has been fired."

My mother stared at her stupidly.

Frau Schneider did not return the glance. She looked down at the wax tablecloth.

"But your husband is a civil servant, isn't he?" asked my mother.

Frau Schneider agreed.

"I thought civil servants couldn't be fired?"

Frau Schneider didn't reply.

"Did he—I mean—did he do something—stupid?" Mother asked.

Frau Schneider shook her head. More tears ran down her face. "They forced him to retire," she finally said. "At *thirty-two!*"

"But why?" Mother asked.

Frau Schneider lifted her head. For a long time she looked at Mother with her cried-out eyes, saying nothing. Then she said, emphasizing each word, "We are Jews, aren't we?"

The Hearing
(1933)

The judge held up the document. "Resch versus Schneider," he called into the court chamber. Then he absorbed himself in the papers in front of him.

The Hearing

An attorney in a wide robe opened the swinging door leading to the witness box. With his eyes he directed Herr Resch out of the public portion of the courtroom and to the witness box.

Herr Schneider stepped alone to the judge's table and waited. If it weren't for his constantly trembling fingers, one would have considered him calm.

Herr Resch's attorney placed himself opposite Herr Schneider.

The judge looked up and quietly instructed the court stenographer about what to take down. After he had done this, he turned to the attorney. "Counsellor," he addressed him, "I miss the legal argument behind your submitted writ of complain. You move on behalf of your client that the apartment now inhabited by the defendant, Herr Schneider, be vacated because of stress on your client, Herr Resch. You do not, however, specify what this stress consists or has consisted of."

The attorney bowed to the judge. His hand gripped his robe and tugged it close over his chest. Leaning back, he began to speak:

"Your Honor. A most extraordinary case is connected with our plea for eviction—but the legal aspect is quite clear. My client lays claim to a right which must surely be granted every German today. We, the plaintiff and I who represent him, are aware that we are treading on virgin ground as far as the law is concerned, but even in Roman law—"

The judge cleared his throat. This created a short pause,

and he interrupted the speaker. "One moment please, Counsellor. Under the statute covering civil suits, we are required to settle the matter at dispute as quickly as possible. If you go back so far into the past, I fear we will need several days. I must, therefore, ask you to present the facts briefly."

Pretending to be conscience-stricken, the attorney lowered his head until his chin touched his chest. Then he leaned back again, tugged at his robe, and began afresh.

I watched, excited. I had never been in a courtroom before. Mother clung to my hand; it was a new experience for her, too. Herr Schneider had asked us to come—"just in case."

In the seat next to Mother crouched Frau Schneider. Her whole body trembled, she was so nervous. Friedrich sat close to her. Eyes wide with fear, he looked in turn at his father, the judge, and the attorney.

"For a year now," the attorney was saying, "my client has been a member of the National Socialist German Workers Party of our highly revered Chancellor of the German Reich, Adolf Hitler." At these words the attorney had snapped to attention and clicked his heels together. Then he resumed his old position and continued to talk.

"My client believes with all his heart in the philosophy of the Nazi party and is convinced of the correctness of its teachings." He stepped back, let go of his robe and pointed an admonishing index finger at the courtroom ceiling. Waving his hand in the air, he continued:

"And a substantial part of the national socialist ideology consists of the rejection of Judaism—Your Honor!"

As if he were dueling, he set one foot forward and pointed at Herr Schneider. He raised his voice: "Your Honor! The defendant is a Jew!"

The attorney fell silent.

The judge looked at the attorney, then at Herr Schneider, and finally at the public.

The attorney began again. In a voice that sounded as if it would break, he imploringly called into the courtroom, "Can my client be expected to keep as a tenant in his house someone whom, according to the basic principles of his party, he must regard as an affliction to his nation, as a constant threat of danger? My client feels the presence of a Jew in his house constitutes a continuous strain under the provisions of the tenant protection law. We therefore move that the accused—"

The judge lifted a finger. "*Defendant* if you please, Counsellor," he corrected. "The defendant!"

Looking contrite, the attorney admitted his error. "Of course, Your Honor, the defendant. I ask your forgiveness." He took a deep breath and continued in an even louder voice than before: "We therefore move that the defendant be instructed to vacate the apartment he now inhabits and that he further be ordered to pay the costs of this hearing."

The judge motioned to the court stenographer. Then he turned to Herr Schneider. "What is your response?"

Frau Schneider moved restlessly back and forth in her

seat. Beside her Friedrich sat stiffly upright. Behind us some spectators whispered to each other. Mother squeezed my hand still harder.

In a firm voice Herr Schneider replied, "I move that the case be dismissed. The plaintiff has always known that I am a Jew. Until a short time ago, he found nothing wrong with that."

The judge bent slightly forward. "How long have you lived in the house of the plaintiff?" he asked.

"For about ten years," was Herr Schneider's reply.

Looking at the attorney, the judge enquired, "Does the defendant speak the truth?"

The attorney tried to catch Herr Resch's eye. "Is this true?" he asked.

Puffing, Herr Resch got up from his bench. Breathing hard, he slowly walked to the front of the courtroom. "Johann Resch," he introduced himself to the judge. "I am the plaintiff."

The stenographer took down his name.

"What do you have to say about this?" the judge asked.

Herr Resch folded his hands over his chest, gasped for air, and began: "I am a convinced National Socialist. Through my own personal effort I want to help accomplish the party's goals. The Jew Schneider prevents me from doing this. His presence in my house will prevent party friends from visiting me. But not only party friends will stay away. My business friends will not come either. Your Honor, this Jew will ruin my business. Every reader of our party newspaper, *Der Stürmer,* knows about the devastating effect of the Jews on our economy."

The judge interrupted Herr Resch. "Just a moment, please. Refrain from giving political speeches, please. Limit yourself to the case at hand. My question is still unanswered. Has the defendant lived in your house for ten years, as he says, and have you always known that he is a Jew?"

Herr Resch stepped closer to the judge's table. "Yes, but you know it was different then. Times have changed. Now I cannot tolerate a Jew in my house!"

The judge waved this aside and said to Herr Resch: "Since you became a member of the NSDAP you cannot tolerate a Jew in your house. Can you assure me that in the near future you may not join a party which is against Catholics or vegetarians? If I accede to your claim today, you may stand before me in a year or two and demand a verdict against another tenant because he is a Catholic or doesn't eat meat."

Herr Resch shook his head. "But that's something quite different . . ."

At this, the attorney gripped his sleeve and pulled him aside. The two spoke together in hushed voices. Herr Resch gesticulated. His attorney kept trying to calm him down.

The judge looked out of the window.

The spectators were talking. Frau Schneider dabbed drops of sweat from her brow. Friedrich stroked her arm.

Finally the attorney walked to the judge's table and

Herr Resch left the courtroom. "My client has empowered me to retract his claim," he declared. "He will bear the costs."

With a bang the judge closed the folder. From the pile in front of him he picked up a new one and prepared to call the next two parties.

Herr Schneider bowed to the judge.

All at once Friedrich cried out. Frau Schneider put her hand over his mouth.

Everyone looked at us. The judge took off his glasses and his eyes searched the courtroom. "Who was that?" he asked.

"My son!" Herr Schneider answered.

"Come up here, my boy!" the judge called.

Herr Schneider collected Friedrich and led him to the judge's table.

Friedrich was still crying.

"Why are you crying, eh?" the judge asked warmly. "You don't have to worry. Nothing will happen to you. That's why I am here, to see that justice is done."

Friedrich wiped his eyes and said, "*You,* yes!"

In the Department Store
(1933)

Friedrich wore a new suit. Like a dancer he pirouetted before me, showing off.

Even my Sunday suit didn't look as fine as that. "Where did you get it?" I asked.

Friedrich laughed, then took my hand and led me down the street.

"Where are you going?" I asked and pulled my hand away.

"Come and see!" he said. "I'll show you something. You'll be amazed!"

Curious, I followed.

We crossed the Ringstrasse, wound our way through a narrow alley and came to the market square. Friedrich pressed forward, not giving me time to glance in the store windows. We left the square through the arcade and turned into the main street.

Grinning, Friedrich greeted the man outside the District Council building with, "Heil Hitler!"

Standing at attention, the man returned the greeting.

Then we entered the Herschel Meyer department store through the main entrance.

FRIEDRICH

A big man in a blue coat and blue cap, with silver braid dangling from his shoulders, tore open the door and bowed low to us.

The lights of the enormous chandelier on the main floor were multiplied many times over in the mirrors around the walls. At our approach, the saleswomen stood up expectantly behind their tables.

Friedrich would not let himself be distracted. Sure of his destination he steered me toward the up escalator. In one bound he leaped on and motioned me to follow.

I placed my feet carefully. When I had a secure footing on the moving steps, I climbed after him. But before I could catch up, Friedrich was already on the second escalator.

He was waiting for me beneath the sign: 3RD FLOOR/ TOYS. He took my hand and led me to a spot where I could overlook the whole department. "Now, what do you see?" he asked proudly.

I peered around me. Everywhere were tables laden with toys. Building blocks, rocking horses, drums, dolls, roller skates, and bicycles. In the midst of it all stood the saleswomen. A few customers wandered among the tables or were being waited on. A gentleman in a black frock coat and gray-striped trousers strolled up and down; here he instructed a saleswoman; there he put a toy back in its proper place.

"I don't know," I said.

"Come, I'll help you," Friedrich said, grabbing my shoulder. Past dolls' carriages, hoops, and metal boats he pulled me along until we stood close behind the gentleman in the black frock coat.

Something about the gentleman struck me as familiar. Suddenly Friedrich coughed.

The gentleman turned around.

It was Herr Schneider!

Herr Schneider laughed, seized Friedrich's elbows and lifted him up. Then he said hello to me and asked, "Well, whom do you like better, the post-office official Schneider or the department head?"

Hesitantly, I said: "You look so elegant."

Herr Schneider laughed again. "I for one like myself better this way." He rubbed his hands. Then he piloted us through the tables to a vast platform.

The platform was one enormous train set. Rails led over mountains and through valleys. Several trains could run at the same time and stop one after the other at the toy station.

Herr Schneider explained how it all worked, then let us play with the trains. He stood and watched. Friedrich controlled the freight trains; I took over the express trains. We almost had a collision, but Herr Schneider prevented it.

While I was attaching a car, he asked me out of the blue, "How is the *Jungvolk*?"

I looked at Friedrich.

"Friedrich told me everything," Herr Schneider explained.

And I replied: "I like it. We are going on a real trip

soon. Maybe I'll be allowed to go. I am already saving money. It'll be great. We'll sleep in tents and cook our own food. I wish Friedrich could join us!"

Herr Schneider looked into the distance and focused on something. He nodded imperceptively. In a near whisper, he said, "A pity, but I guess it's better so!"

Silently Friedrich and I played on.

Herr Schneider walked up and down behind us. Suddenly he asked another question: "What does your father say about the *Jungvolk?*"

I turned around. "Father is glad I like it in the *Jungvolk*. He makes sure I go on duty regularly and punctually, especially since he joined the party."

Herr Schneider looked at me, frightened. "So your father's also in the party now?"

I nodded. "Yes, he thinks it can only be good for us."

Herr Schneider sighed. He turned away. After a while he called: "Fräulein Ewert, please come over here a moment!"

A young salesgirl hurried over.

"These two young gentlemen," Herr Schneider told her, "these two *customers,* Fräulein Ewert, would like to see our toy exhibition. Kindly show them everything they would like to see and explain what needs explaining. And after the tour, each young man may choose a toy for one mark and carry it off—but one mark is the limit, understood? I'll take care of the bill. Please, Fräulein Ewert, guide the gentlemen!"

Fräulein Ewert nodded, smiling.

Herr Schneider shook hands. "*Auf Wiedersehen,* boys, and have fun!" Slowly he walked away. At the fourth table, he turned and waved, but he was no longer smiling.

The Teacher
(1934)

The school bell rang. At the last tone, Teacher Neudorf closed the book and stood up. Slowly, in thought, he walked toward us. He cleared his throat and said: "The lesson is over—but please stay a little longer; I want to tell you a story. Anyone who wants to can go home, though."

We looked at each other quizzically.

Herr Neudorf stepped to the window, turning his back to us. From his jacket pocket he drew a pipe and began to fill it, looking at the trees in the schoolyard all the while.

Noisily we collected our things. We prepared our brief-cases and satchels. But no one left the classroom. We all waited.

Awkwardly, Herr Neudorf lit his pipe. With obvious enjoyment he blew a few puffs against the windows. Only then did he turn to face us. He surveyed the rows of seats.

FRIEDRICH

When he saw that all were still filled, he nodded to us with a smile.

All eyes focused on Herr Neudorf. We didn't talk. From the hall came the sounds of the other classes. In one of the back benches someone shuffled his feet.

Herr Neudorf walked to the front row. He sat on one of the desks. His pipe glowing, he looked at each of us in turn and blew the smoke over our heads to the window.

We stared at our teacher, tense and expectant.

At last he began to speak in a calm, soft voice. "Lately, you've heard a lot about Jews, haven't you?" We nodded. "Well, today I also have a reason to talk to you about Jews."

We leaned forward to hear better. A few propped their chins on their schoolbags. There wasn't a sound.

Herr Neudorf directed a blue cloud of sweet-smelling smoke up to the ceiling. After a pause, he continued, "Two thousand years ago all Jews lived in the land which is now called Palestine; the Jews call it Israel.

"The Romans governed the country through their governors and prefects. But the Jews did not want to submit to foreign rule and they rebelled against the Romans. The Romans smashed the uprising and in the year 70 after the birth of Christ destroyed the Second Temple in Jerusalem. The leaders of the revolt were banished to Spain or the Rhineland. A generation later, the Jews dared to rise again. This time the Romans razed Jerusalem to the ground. The Jews fled or were banished. They scattered over the whole earth.

"Years passed. Many gained wealth and standing. Then came the Crusades.

"Heathens had conquered the Holy Land and kept Christians from the holy places. Eloquent priests demanded the liberation of the Holy Grave; inflamed by their words, thousands of people assembled.

"But some declared, 'What is the use of marching against the infidels in the Holy Land while there are infidels living in our midst?'

"Thus began the persecution of the Jews. In many places they were herded together; they were murdered and burned. They were dragged by force to be baptized; those who refused were tortured.

"Hundreds of Jews took their own lives to escape massacre. Those who could escape did so.

"When the Crusades were over, impoverished sovereigns who had taken part in them had their Jewish subjects imprisoned and executed without trials and claimed their possessions.

"Again, many Jews fled, this time to the East. They found refuge in Poland and Russia. But in the last century, there, too, they began to be persecuted.

"The Jews were forced to live in ghettos, in isolated sections of towns. They were not allowed to take up so-called 'honest' professions: they could not become craftsmen nor were they allowed to own houses or land. They were only allowed to work in trade and at moneylending."

The teacher paused, his pipe had gone out. He placed it in the groove for pens and pencils. He got off the desk and wandered about the classroom. He polished his glasses and continued:

"The Old Testament of the Christians is also the Holy Scripture of the Jews; they call it Torah, which means 'instruction.' In the Torah is written down what God commanded Moses. The Jews have thought a great deal about the Torah and its commandments. How the laws of the Torah are to be interpreted they have put down in another very great work—the Talmud, which means 'study.'

"Orthodox Jews still live by the law of the Torah. And that is not easy. The Torah, for instance, forbids the Jew to light a fire on the Sabbath or to eat the meat of unclean animals such as pigs.

"The Torah prophesies the Jews' fate. If they break the holy laws, they will be persecuted and must flee, until the Messiah leads them back to their Promised Land, there to create His Kingdom among them. Because Jews did not believe Jesus to be the true Messiah, because they regarded him as an impostor like many before him, they crucified him. And to this day many people have not forgiven them for this. They believe the most absurd things about Jews; some only wait for the day when they can persecute them again.

"There are many people who do not like Jews. Jews strike them as strange and sinister; they believe them capable of everything bad just because they don't know them well enough!"

Attentively we followed the account. It was so quiet

that we could hear the soles of Herr Neudorf's shoes creak. Everyone looked at him; only Friedrich looked down at his hands.

"Jews are accused of being crafty and sly. How could they be anything else? Someone who must always live in fear of being tormented and hunted must be very strong in his soul to remain an upright human being.

"It is claimed that the Jews are avaricious and deceitful. Must they not be both? Again and again, they have been robbed and dispossessed; again and again, they had to leave everything they owned behind. They have discovered that in case of need money is the only way to secure life and safety.

"But one thing even the worst Jew-haters have to concede—the Jews are a very capable people! Only able people can survive two thousand years of persecution.

"By always accomplishing more and doing it better than the people they lived among, the Jews gained esteem and importance again and again. Many great scholars and artists were and are Jews.

"If today, or tomorrow, you should see Jews being mistreated, reflect on one thing—Jews are human beings, human beings like us!"

Without glancing at us, Herr Neudorf took up his pipe. He scraped the ashes out of the bowl and lit the remaining tobacco. After a few puffs, he said, "Now I am sure you will want to know why I have told you all this, eh?"

He walked to Friedrich's seat and put a hand on his shoulder.

"One of us will leave our school today. It appears that Friedrich Schneider may no longer come to our school; he must change to a Jewish school because he is of the Jewish faith.

"That Friedrich has to attend a Jewish school is no punishment, but only a change. I hope you will understand that and remain Friedrich's friends, just as I will remain his friend even though he will no longer be in my class. Friedrich may need good friends."

Herr Neudorf turned Friedrich around by his shoulder. "I wish you all the best, Friedrich!" the teacher said, "and *Auf Wiedersehen!*"

Friedrich bent his head. In a low voice he replied, *"Auf Wiedersehen!"*

With quick steps Herr Neudorf hurried to the front of the class. He jerked up his right arm, the hand straight out at eye level, and said: "Heil Hitler!"

We jumped up and returned the greeting in the same way.

The Cleaning Lady
(1935)

Ever since Herr Schneider had become head of the toy department of Herschel Meyer, Frau Penk came to the

Schneiders twice a week. She helped Frau Schneider with the cleaning and other housework.

After my father not only found work but also was promoted because of his membership in the Party, Frau Penk also helped my mother.

Frau Penk was hardworking and thorough; one could recommend her to others without hesitation. Frau Penk took on as many jobs as she could possibly handle. She liked families with children best because she didn't have any herself. Because her husband returned from the factory very late in the evening, because she was bored being at home by herself, because she loved buying things, that's why Frau Penk cleaned for other people.

It was a Wednesday in the fall of 1935. I was doing my homework, and Frau Penk was cleaning our windows, when the doorbell rang. I heard Mother going to the door, and then Frau Schneider's voice asking after Frau Penk.

Frau Penk heard this too. She had put down the window cloth when Mother returned to the room with Frau Schneider and Friedrich.

"I wanted to see you," said Frau Schneider, and held out her hand to Frau Penk. "I wanted to ask if you could please come a little later on Friday. I have to take Friedrich to the doctor, you see," she added, and only then asked, "Is that all right with you, Frau Penk?"

Frau Penk looked upset. She had taken a handkerchief from her apron pocket and was twisting it between her fingers. She kept her eyes on the handkerchief. After a while she said: "I would have come up later, because I wanted to talk to you anyway, Frau Schneider." She paused, then looked straight at Frau Schneider and said, "You know, Frau Schneider . . . you must understand that . . . my husband thinks . . . I really have enjoyed working for you . . . and I like Friedrich so much, you see . . ."

Frau Schneider blushed furiously. She lowered her head. Her hands played restlessly with her coat buttons. She breathed quickly.

Puzzled, Mother looked at Frau Schneider and at Frau Penk. It was clear from her face that she didn't understand what was going on.

Frau Penk pulled Friedrich to her. She put her arm round his neck, pressing him tightly against her while her left hand continually smoothed her apron.

Equally puzzled, Friedrich stared at his mother, then at Frau Penk.

Frau Schneider lifted her head. She swallowed, cleared her throat, and said: "It's all right, Frau Penk. I know what you mean, and I am not angry with you. I thank you for helping us so well for so long. I wish you all the best!" Quickly she offered Frau Penk her hand, called to Friedrich, and hurriedly left our apartment.

When Mother came back from the door, she shrugged her shoulders. "I no longer understand anything!" she declared.

Frau Penk still stood in the same spot and kneaded her handkerchief.

"Did you quarrel with Frau Schneider?" Mother asked

her. "What's going on? How could you give up such a family, such a good family?"

Frau Penk turned her back toward Mother. She picked up the window cloth. Wiping the window frame, she addressed the wall, "What can I do? Do you think I *liked* doing it? But I'm only twenty-eight, you see."

Mother pulled a face, as if Frau Penk had given her a riddle to solve. "What on earth has the fact that you're only twenty-eight got to do with it?"

Over her shoulder Frau Penk peered at my mother in astonishment. "But don't you know about the new law the Nazis have passed?" she asked in a superior tone of voice.

"No!"

"Jews and non-Jews are no longer allowed to marry. All marriages between Jews and non-Jews are dissolved. And non-Jewish women who are under thirty-five are no longer allowed to work in the houses of Jews."

"My God!" sighed Mother.

"Last week," Frau Penk went on, "I saw a young woman being paraded through town. Around her neck she wore a sign that said:

> I DESERVE A BEATING FROM YOU
> BECAUSE I LOVE A JEW!"

Mother covered her face with her hands. "But that's terrible!" she wailed.

"Do you think I want to be driven through town like

(67)

that, or maybe even land in prison?" Frau Penk shook her head.

Slowly Mother went to the door. Before she left the room, she stopped and asked, "And what does your husband say to all that, Frau Penk?"

Frau Penk folded the window cloth. "You know," she said softly, "I would have known how to arrange it all right. But my husband used to be a communist and he feels we ought to be careful and not do anything wrong."

Reasons
(1936)

Father returned late from a Party meeting. Tired, he glanced at the clock. To Mother he said, "I don't want to eat just yet."

Mother looked puzzled, but lifted the pot off the stove.

Father took a chair and put it close to the door in the hall. By the hall light he read the newspaper.

Mother looked after him from the kitchen door. With a sigh she went back to work.

Father scanned the newspaper very absent-mindedly. Each time there was a sound anywhere in the house, he opened the door a crack.

I had stopped playing long before. From the living room I watched Father's strange behavior and wondered what it might mean.

When he recognized Herr Schneider's footsteps on the stairs, my father wrenched open the door. He flung the newspaper to the floor and stepped out onto the landing.

Herr Schneider was climbing the stairs slowly, Friedrich at his side; Friedrich was carrying his father's briefcase. My father barred their way.

Both looked at him in astonishment.

"Herr Schneider," Father said in a muffled voice, "may I ask you to come in for a moment?"

Herr Schneider asked: "Can Friedrich come, too?"

Father agreed. He led them both into our living room. He offered Herr Schneider a seat by the window, assigning Friedrich to me.

Friedrich and I quietly played dominoes in the corner by the stove.

Father gave Herr Schneider one of his good Sunday cigars; he lit a cigarette for himself. The two smoked in silence for a while before they began.

"I find it difficult, Herr Schneider!" Father murmured finally, then he said in a slightly louder voice: "May I speak freely and openly?" He looked Herr Schneider straight in the eye.

Herr Schneider's face had grown very serious. At first, he hesitated. "I beg you to," he finally replied. The hand holding the cigar trembled slightly; specks of ash floated onto his trousers and the floor.

(69)

Guiltily, Father looked at the floor. In a whisper, he told Herr Schneider, "I have joined the Party."

Equally softly and in a voice that sounded a little disappointed, Herr Schneider returned, "I know!"

Surprised, Father lifted his head.

"Your son has told me," Herr Schneider explained. "And," his voice was sad, "I would have guessed it anyway."

Father looked at me reproachfully. He puffed at his cigarette. Quietly he went on: "You must understand, Herr Schneider, that I was out of work for a long time. Since Hitler's in power, I have work again—better work than I had ever hoped for. We are doing well."

Herr Schneider tried to break in. Soothingly, he said, "You don't have to apologize; really you don't."

Father brushed this aside. "This year for the first time we can take a vacation trip together," he went on. "Through the Party travel bureau. In the meantime I've already been offered another good position, and all because I am a member of the Party. Herr Schneider, I have become a member of the NSDAP because I believe it's of advantage to my family and myself."

Herr Schneider interrupted my father. "I understand you very, very well. Perhaps—if I weren't a Jew—perhaps I would have acted just like you. But I am a Jew."

Father lit another cigarette. "I don't by any means agree with the Party in everything it does and demands. But then, Herr Schneider, doesn't every party and every leadership have its dark side?"

Herr Schneider smiled painfully. "And, unfortunately, I stand in the shadows this time."

"That's why I have asked you to come in, Herr Schneider," Father again took up the conversation. "That's what I wanted to talk to you about."

Herr Schneider said nothing. He just looked at Father; there was no sign of fear in his eyes. His hand no longer trembled, and he breathed evenly. He smoked his cigar with obvious enjoyment.

Friedrich had pushed the dominoes aside long ago. He was listening intently. His eyes seemed incredibly large, but one could easily believe that they were looking at something far away. He seemed not to notice that I was there. I listened, too. Even though I didn't understand everything, I was touched by the seriousness of their conversation.

"You know, Herr Schneider," my father began again, "I went to a Party meeting this afternoon. At such meetings one gets to hear a lot about the plans and aims of the leadership, and if one knows how to listen properly, one can add quite a bit besides.

"I want to ask you, Herr Schneider, why are you and your family still here?"

Herr Schneider looked astonished.

But Father was already going on: "Many of those who share your faith have already left Germany because life was made too hard for them here. And it will only get worse! Think of your family, Herr Schneider, and go away!"

Herr Schneider gave my father his hand. "I thank you for your frankness," he said, "and I appreciate it fully. You see, I, too, have wondered if it wouldn't be better to flee Germany. There are reasons against it."

Excitedly, my father interrupted: "Everything, but everything points toward your going today rather than tomorrow. Why can't you grasp that, Herr Schneider?"

My father lit his third cigarette. Usually he smoked no more than five cigarettes during the whole day.

"These are my reasons," Herr Schneider continued. "I am German, my wife is German, my son is German, all our relatives are German. What could we do abroad? How would we be received? Do you seriously think they like us Jews better elsewhere? And anyway, it will all quiet down eventually. Now that the year of the Olympics has begun, we're hardly bothered. Don't you agree?"

Flicking off the ash, Father broke his cigarette. At once, he pulled another from the pack. He listened to Herr Schneider with a skeptical expression, then said, "Don't trust to the peace, Herr Schneider."

"There has been prejudice against us for two thousand years," Herr Schneider said. "No one must expect this prejudice to disappear in half a century of living together peacefully. We Jews must learn to accept that. In the Middle Ages those prejudices threatened our lives. Human beings must surely have become a little more reasonable by now."

Father frowned. "You talk as if all you had to fear was a small group of Jew-haters. But your opponent is a government!" Father turned the cigarette between his fingers and took another puff.

"But surely that's our good fortune!" retorted Herr Schneider. "Our freedom may be curtailed and we may be treated unfairly, but at least we don't have to fear that the people will murder us pitilessly."

Father shrugged. "Are you just going to accept slavery and injustice?"

Herr Schneider leaned forward. He spoke calmly and with assurance. "God has given us Jews a task. We must fulfill that task. We have always been persecuted—ever since we were exiled. I have given much thought to this lately. Perhaps we'll manage to put an end to our wandering by not seeking flight any more, by learning to suffer, by staying where we are."

Father put out his cigarette. "I admire your faith, Herr Schneider," he said, "but I cannot share it. I can't do more than advise you to go away!"

Herr Schneider stood up. "What you envisage cannot be, not in the twentieth century! But I thank you for your frankness and for your concern for us." And again he shook hands with my father.

Father accompanied him to the door.

Herr Schneider motioned to Friedrich. In our hall they stopped again. "And if you should turn out to be right after all," Herr Schneider said in a very low voice, "may I ask you to do something?"

Father nodded.

"If something should happen to me," he said, and it

(73)

came out faintly and haltingly, "if something should happen to me, please look after my wife and son!"

Father felt for Herr Schneider's hand and pressed it hard.

In the Swimming Pool
(1938)

It was hot. No one who didn't have to went outside. Only a few people dragged themselves, sweating, through whatever shade they could find.

We had arranged to meet outside the town where the woods began and then cycle together to the swimming pool.

Mother had loaned me her bicycle. It didn't look beautiful any more, but it still worked very well.

Friedrich arrived on his shining new blue bicycle. Not only was the bicycle new; he had polished it as well. On the way to the forest pool we sang hiking songs like "Waldeslust" and Friedrich let go of his handlebars. His bicycle swung from one side of the road to the other.

Suddenly a man approached on a silvery bicycle that gleamed in the sun. Even Friedrich's bike couldn't compare with that.

Despite the heat the other cyclist seemed to be in a great

hurry. He rang his bell when he was still far away because Friedrich was still swinging back and forth across the road.

Friedrich gripped his handlebars but otherwise paid no attention to the man. He forced him to brake hard.

Which the stranger did, swearing loudly.

Only at the last possible moment did Friedrich clear the way. The cyclist rode on, pedaling furiously. Friedrich whistled after him through his fingers. Far from turning around, the stranger only pushed harder on the pedals and sped down the path.

A quarter of an hour later we reached the forest swimming pool. We chained our bikes to a tree. After getting undressed, we handed in our things and received tags with numbers in exchange. Friedrich tied his to his ankle and jumped into the water. He could swim much better than I, and he was an excellent diver.

I showered first. Then I carefully went down the stairs into the cold water and swam after Friedrich.

Until late afternoon we played in the water and let ourselves be broiled by the sun. When I finally looked at the big clock over the entrance, we had already stayed past our time. We were going to collect our clothes when Friedrich couldn't find his tag.

He ran back and dived to the bottom of the pool, but he didn't find the tag. Shrugging his shoulders, he joined the line of other boys waiting to get their things. They were slow at the checkout counter. The attendant was very busy.

FRIEDRICH

I was ahead of Friedrich and received my hanger first. I changed quickly. When I came out of the locker room, Friedrich was still standing in line. I wrung out my bathing trunks and wrapped them in my towel.

Finally the attendant turned to Friedrich. He scolded him when he heard what had happened. But then he let Friedrich come to the other side of the counter. Shivering with cold and accompanied by the sullen attendant, Friedrich searched for his things.

The attendant was about to let him wait until after he had tended to the waiting boys when Friedrich shouted: "There they are!" The attendant took down the hanger he pointed to and carried it to the counter. There he hung it from a hook. "What's your name?" he asked.

"Friedrich Schneider."

"Where's your ID?"

"In the right back trouser pocket. The button's loose."

The attendant looked for the pocket, unbuttoned it, and pulled out the case with the identification card. Then he took out the card and looked at it.

Friedrich still stood before the counter, his teeth chattering. He looked at the ground and seemed embarrassed.

All of a sudden the attendant whistled loudly through his teeth.

From the other side came the female attendant.

"Just take a look at this!" the attendant said. "You won't get to see many more of them." Everyone could hear his explanation: "This is one of the Jewish identification cards. The scoundrel lied to me. He claims his name's Friedrich

Schneider—it's Friedrich *Israel* Schneider, that's what it is—a Jew that's what he is! A Jew in our swimming pool!" He looked disgusted.

All those still waiting for their clothes stared at Friedrich.

As if he could no longer bear to touch it, the attendant threw Friedrich's identification card and its case across the counter. "Think of it! Jewish things among the clothes of respectable human beings!" he screamed, flinging the coat hanger holding Friedrich's clothes on the ground so they scattered in all directions.

While Friedrich collected his things, the attendant announced, "Now I'll have to wash my hands before I can go on with my work. Ugh!" He walked away from the counter, kicking one of Friedrich's shoes into a blocked-up foot bath.

He returned before Friedrich found all his things.

"It's your affair where you get dressed," he snarled at him. "You won't get into our changing rooms."

Helpless and still damp, Friedrich clutched his clothes. He searched for a place where he could dry himself and get dressed. There was no protected corner, and he hastily rubbed himself with his towel and pulled his trousers on over the wet bathing trunks. Water dripping from his trouser legs, he left the swimming pool.

The attendant was still screaming, but we could no longer understand what he was saying.

I had already unlocked our bikes.

Friedrich fastened his things on the luggage carrier. He

didn't dare look into my eyes. Quietly he said, "I'll dress properly in the woods."

Then we heard an uproar behind us. "This is where it was!" said a big boy. "I'm quite sure this is where I locked it. I've searched everywhere, but it's gone. It was all silver; I'd just polished it, too."

A lot of curious boys quickly collected. They gave advice: "Follow the trail!" "Inform the police!"

Friedrich pricked up his ears. He left his bicycle and walked to the circle that had formed around the boy whose bike had been stolen. "You there," Friedrich said to him, "I know who stole your bike. I saw the man who did it; I can describe him in detail."

Everyone looked at Friedrich. A lane formed between him and the owner of the silver bike.

The boy stepped closer to Friedrich. "Say," he asked, "aren't you the Jew from the pool a while back?" Friedrich blushed, lowered his eyes to the ground. "You don't think the police would believe you, do you?"

The Festival
(1938)

Friedrich had met me on the street. "Come," he'd said, making me curious, "you'll see something very special!"

The Festival

I had gone with him, even though I had to keep thinking of my father. Only a week ago he had begged me, "Don't show yourself so often with the Schneiders; otherwise, I'll have difficulties."

Now we stood in the large room of the synagogue, Herr Schneider, Friedrich, and I. Friedrich and his father wore their best suits, while I looked shabby in my everyday clothes.

Gradually, the bench in front of us filled up. Men with hats on their heads shook hands with us and wished us *"Gut Shabbes."* All found an extra word of kindness for Friedrich or patted his shoulder.

One by one, everyone lifted his seat, revealing a small compartment underneath.

Friedrich took a large white scarf from his, as well as a prayer book and his *yarmulke,* exchanging the latter for his cap. He touched the fringed scarf with his lips and draped it around his shoulders.

"My *tallis,* my prayer shawl," he whispered to me.

A man wearing a black hat and a long black coat that reached to his feet walked to a podium in the center of the room. The podium was covered with a carpet. He opened a thick book from the back and immediately began to chant a prayer.

"Our rabbi!" Friedrich informed me in a low voice. Then he, too, opened his prayer book and prayed in Hebrew. From time to time he interrupted the rabbi's prayer with an interjection, and at one point, he seemed to start a completely different prayer.

(79)

FRIEDRICH

I was astonished. How did Friedrich know Hebrew so well? He had never told me anything about it. Suddenly he seemed like one of the many adults around us. From time to time he looked up from his prayer book and nodded to me.

The rabbi prayed facing the east. Swaying back and forth, he kept making small bows to the east wall which was covered with a red curtain.

This curtain was embroidered with Hebrew characters. Otherwise, there wasn't a single picture in the room, no ornament, only large, many-branched candelabra with candles in them. From a side balcony, the women watched the service.

While I was still examining the inside of the synagogue, the voices of the congregation merged with the rabbi's. The chant grew louder.

With measured steps the rabbi walked to the curtain. The red velvet was pulled aside. Behind it, a small door in the wall could be seen.

The rabbi opened the door, then stood aside so everyone could look into the box.

"That's our Torah inside the Ark," Friedrich explained.

The Torah was wrapped in a cloth decorated with a silver crown and shield.

The rabbi lifted the heavy scrolls out of the Ark. In solemn procession he carried them through the synagogue. Wherever he passed, members of the congregation left their seats, touched the Torah with their *talaysim* and then touched the *talaysim* to their lips.

"Now comes the surprise," Friedrich told me. He seemed very excited.

Herr Schneider pulled Friedrich to him and soothingly patted his shoulder and stroked his hair.

At the podium, the crown, the shield, and the cloth were removed from the Torah and the great parchment placed on the podium. One after the other the rabbi called seven congregants to the podium. Then he called Friedrich.

Herr Schneider put both hands on his shoulder. Proudly, he looked into his son's eyes before sending him on his way.

The rabbi also greeted Friedrich much more solemnly than he had the men before him.

"For the first time in his life he's been called to read the weekly section!" Herr Schneider proudly told me. "Afterward he's also permitted to read a section from the Prophets."

Like the men before him, Friedrich touched the Torah with his *tallis* as instructed by the rabbi, then kissed the *tallis*. Then he recited the Blessing. But while the prayer leader had chanted a Torah section with each of the men before him, Friedrich took over the silver staff, led it along the lines from right to left, and chanted his section of the Torah by himself.

When he had read his section quickly and surely, he touched the last passage once more with his *tallis* and the *tallis* with his lips.

While the scrolls of the Torah were again wrapped in their ornaments, Friedrich read the section from the

FRIEDRICH

Prophets from a large book. Then he returned to his seat. Just as at the beginning of the service, the rabbi carried the Torah in procession through the synagogue, and again the congregants pressed toward it.

The rabbi replaced the Torah in the Ark and said another prayer before closing the little door.

Then he gave a short sermon. For the first time since I had entered the synagogue, he spoke in German. The sermon was directed solely at Friedrich; it singled him out before the whole congregation.

Men kept looking at Friedrich, nodding to him with smiles of well-wishes.

"Today, a week after your thirteenth birthday," the rabbi said, "you have, for the first time in your life, been called upon to read a section from the Torah. This is an honor for every Jew, but the day on which this happens for the first time is a special day. With it begins a new phase of your life. From now on you alone will be responsible to the Lord our God for your deeds. Until this day, your father has borne this responsibility, but from now on, you stand among us as an equal member of this congregation. Remember that!

"Obey the commandments of the Lord! No one can take away your guilt if you break them.

"You are assuming a difficult duty in a difficult time. We are chosen by the Lord our God to be guided back into our homeland by the Messiah and there to help found His Kingdom. But God has placed the heavy burden of persecution upon us until that day.

(82)

The Festival

"We must continually remind ourselves that the Lord our God has determined this fate. We must not and cannot escape it, not even when we feel we will collapse under it. Reflect, the Holy Torah demands . . . " and the rabbi finished his sermon with a sentence in Hebrew.

Soon afterward the service closed with a communal song.

I waited outside the synagogue for Friedrich and his father. There were so many questions I was burning to ask. But there was no opportunity. All the men from the congregation came over and congratulated Friedrich. One could see how proud he felt.

After the women also had left the synagogue, we went home in a flock of relatives and friends.

Frau Schneider had run ahead. She received us by the door and led us all into the living room, where she had arranged a festive Sabbath feast. There was plenty of everything.

But before the feast could begin, Friedrich gave a speech, just like a grown-up orator. "Dear Father, dear Mother, dear relations," he began. "The Lord has ordered us to honor Father and Mother so that we may long live in the land that he has given us. May he forgive me for not following his commandment sufficiently until this day.

"For thirteen years, dear parents, you have instructed me and guided me in the commandments of our Lord, through good times and bad times. It is thanks to you who have stood by me that I have today been received into the congregation. In my thoughts and my deeds I will show myself worthy of this honor and duty.

"May the Lord grant you, dear parents and relations, a hundred and twenty years of healthy and joyful life, so that I may find time to repay the thanks that I owe you. . . ."

Frau Schneider wept.

Herr Schneider looked at the floor, absent-mindedly rummaging in his jacket pocket.

When Friedrich finished his speech, everyone applauded, and his father presented him with a wristwatch. The other guests had brought presents, too.

"Tell me," I asked Friedrich in a whisper, "where did you learn all that, the Hebrew and the speech?"

Friedrich smiled proudly. "Learned it. Had to practice my Torah section and the speech for almost three months."

I showed my astonishment.

Friedrich enjoyed it. "Shall I tell you what Friedrich is in Hebrew?" he asked me.

I nodded.

"Solomon!" Friedrich told me, laughing.

While we ate, the doorbell rang.

"I wonder who would come this late?" Frau Schneider asked, puzzled. She went to the door and opened it.

Herr Neudorf, his former teacher, came into the room. He wished Friedrich all the best on his Bar Mitzvah. Then he gave him a fountain pen. Friedrich's name had been engraved in gold on the cap.

The Encounter
(1938)

Our physical education teacher was Herr Schuster. Herr Schuster was also a commander of storm troopers, and in the First World War he had been a captain. All who knew him feared his severity. Anyone who disobeyed him, or perhaps changed too slowly, was forced to do knee bends until he collapsed. We all kept out of his way if we could. Physical education as Herr Schuster understood it consisted primarily of marches—forced marches, marches with full pack, and whatever other marches he could think of.

One day just before our double gym lesson he came into our classroom. "No break today!" he announced. "You'll get enough fresh air without it—we're going on a forced march."

Our faces fell. But no one dared object, not even Karl Meisen who'd sprained his ankle after a daredevil jump during our last gym lesson.

"Everyone empty their briefcases and satchels!" ordered Herr Schuster. "Notebooks and textbooks under your desks!" Obediently we did as told.

"Form one line in the yard, the last man to stand three

steps from the chestnut tree. Take your briefcases and satchels. Quick, march!" The order echoed through our classroom.

We picked up our satchels and briefcases. We raced down the stairs to avoid being late.

Herr Schuster already stood in the yard. We looked for our places in the line. "Fall in line is what I said!" he barked at us. "That means 'at attention!' " He took a deep breath. "To the wall, quick, march!"

We dashed toward the wall, but he stopped us with an "Attention!" before we could reach it. We had to fall in line once more, again rush the wall, again assemble. Then, marching in formation, we moved toward the gym.

Bricks, left by a construction firm ages ago, were stacked against the gym wall. Herr Schuster now stuffed these bricks into our briefcases and satchels.

"My briefcase is larger than the others', they only got two bricks!" Franz Schulten complained as Herr Schuster loaded three into his bag and added yet another.

The owners of briefcases usually patronized the satchel bearers, but today they were envied because they could carry their loads on their backs. We fell into march formation and went off.

Still inside the school district, where parents might be watching, Herr Schuster had us sing a song: " 'Siehst du im Osten' (Do you see in the East), second verse!"

When the last of the column shouted: "Done!" the head roared back: "Three——four!"

And we began again:

The Encounter

"Many years have gone their way,
with our nation enslaved and defrauded.
Traitors and Jews out of this made their gain,
asking the sacrifice of legions.
Then to our people
a Führer was born,
who restored
hope and faith to our people.
Germany to arms! Germany to arms!"

With the heavy bricks in our packs weighing us down,
we used up our last breath. But we had barely left the district when we were ordered to continue double time. We
circled half our town like that.

An hour and a half later we dragged ourselves back
into our school district. The handle of Franz Schulten's
case had broken; he carried his case full of bricks on his
shoulder. His jacket was soaked through with sweat.

Karl Meisen, with his sprained ankle, had been left
behind, crying. The rest of us could hardly walk straight.

But Herr Schuster strode at our side, erect and at ease.
He smiled mockingly whenever he caught one of us limp-
ing.

In this condition we encountered another class. At first
we didn't recognize anyone, but then we discovered Friedrich. It was a class from the Jewish school.

Herr Schuster had also spied Friedrich. "Boys!" he said
crisply. "Now we'll show them over there what German
boys are made of. You're not going to let yourselves be
ridiculed by those inferior Jews, are you? I expect perfect

timing. Is that understood?" He marched along the column and pushed us weary marchers back into line.

We made a gigantic effort to pull ourselves together, straightened up.

Herr Schuster ordered a song.

Eyes staring fixedly ahead, laden down but erect, we marched past the Jewish class and belted out:

> "Crooked Jews are marching along,
> they're marching through the Red Sea.
> The waves close over them,
> and the world is at peace!"

The Pogrom
(1938)

It was around one o'clock when I came out of school.

Dr. Askenase's name plate lay bent outside his door. The frame of his office window dangled over the coal chute, hanging from the cord of the rolling shutters. Someone had thrown all his instruments and medicines onto the street.

The stink of the smashed medicine bottles polluted the whole area. A radio that had been hacked to bits stuck fast in a manhole.

From where I was, I could see that broken glass was

strewn as far along the road as the shop belonging to Abraham Rosenthal, the little Jew with the pointed beard.

Counter and broken shelves were piled high on the sidewalk like garbage.

The wind blew dirty sheets of paper against the wall.

Some adults rummaged among the things. From time to time some bent down and furtively stuck something in their bags.

I looked down into the little basement shop. Wallpaper hung in shreds from the walls. The floor was knee-high in torn colored paper, ruined notebooks, unwound rolls of colored ribbon, torn drawing pads, crumpled photos, smeared dress patterns, pieces of candy, and sticks of licorice.

At the next corner I ran into a troop of five men and three women. They were armed with crowbars, wore helmets and headscarves. Silently they were heading for a Jewish home for apprentices.

Many curious hangers-on were following them.

"About time, too, that they get what's coming to them," commented a little man with glasses. "They've had it coming to them for a long time. I just hope they don't miss anyone!"

I, too, joined the group.

"Today you'll see something, boy," the little man promised, "that you can tell your grandchildren about."

The group halted outside the Jewish home for apprentices. At first, they all just seemed to stand around. Then they began to mutter and exchange advice, apparently trying to give each other courage. At last, one of the men walked forward.

"Open up!" he shouted to the upper floors of the home.

But nothing stirred, no window opened, not even a curtain moved. The house seemed dead.

The man bawled his order a second time to shut windows.

Our eyes were all glued to the building. I was very excited. What would happen?

Nothing did!

One of the women reviled the Jewish home in an ugly voice.

I couldn't understand what she said because her voice was so shrill.

The man paid no attention to the screeching. With heavy steps he marched toward the heavy oak door. He pressed down the handle, but the door was locked.

He stepped back three, four steps, and threw his back against the door. He tried again, this time taking a longer run.

Again nothing!

Other men from the group joined in. At first singly, then in unison, they threw themselves against the door of the building.

Even the women leaped to their aid.

Only the woman who had been so abusive earlier stayed where she was; she cheered the others on.

Soon her "one—two—three—one—two—three!" resounded through the street.

And in the rhythm of her shouts, men and women hurled themselves against the door.

From the circle of bystanders more and more joined in. Egged on by the woman, they gradually joined her chant. It was then that I caught myself shouting "one—two—three" and edging closer with each shout. All at once I, too, was straining at the door and didn't know how I had gotten there. I also noticed that no one was watching now.

All took part.

Very slowly the door gave way. When it finally burst open, no one expected it. Those in the first row fell into the house. The ones behind them stumbled across the wreckage. The rest crowded in after.

I was pulled along with the throng. When I had a chance to stop and look around me, the sounds of crashing and bumping came from all parts of the house.

As I climbed the stairs with my schoolbag, bedside tables zoomed by and burst apart at the bottom of the stairs.

All this was strangely exhilarating.

No one stopped the destruction. Of the people living in the house, none were to be seen. Nothing but empty corridors, empty rooms.

In one of the bedrooms I came across the woman who had done the shouting. She was slashing open mattresses with a vegetable knife. She smiled at me in a cloud of dust. "Don't you know me any more?" she asked in a squeaky voice.

I thought, then shook my head.

(91)

FRIEDRICH

She laughed out loud. "When I bring you your paper every morning?" With the back of her hand, she wiped her mouth, lifted a bottle of milk to her lips and drank from it. Then she put the bottle down again and whirled the slashed mattress out of the window.

A middle-aged man had come across a tool box. He was stuffing all his pockets, pressed a brand new hammer into my hand.

At first I just played with the hammer. Without paying attention I swung it loosely from my wrist, back and forth, back and forth. At one point I must have nicked something—glass crashed at my blow.

I jumped. The glass had belonged to a bookcase. But almost at once my curiosity awoke. Gently I tapped a cracked pane of glass and it fell out of its frame. By now I was enjoying myself. I swung so hard against the third pane that its splinters fell in bursts to the floor.

With my hammer I cut myself a path through the corridors, smashing aside whatever barred my way: legs of chairs, toppled wardrobes, chamber pots and glassware. I felt so strong! I could have sung I was so drunk with the desire to swing my hammer.

I discovered a door leading to a small classroom that hadn't been touched yet. Curiously, I looked around.

Turning, I hit against a T-square with my schoolbag. It clattered to the floor and I stepped on it by mistake. It burst with a loud bang that sounded like a shot.

I stopped short. Lots more T-squares hung on the wall. I took down another and repeated the bang. This time, the sound was deeper. One after the other, I bent T-squares till they broke. And I enjoyed the fact that each had a different tone to it.

When I couldn't find any more T-squares, I picked up my hammer from the podium. I drummed it along the desktops and searched all the cupboards, desk drawers, and closets in the room. But I found nothing else to satisfy my lust for destruction.

Disappointed, I was about to leave the room, but by the door I looked back one last time. Against the far wall stood a large blackboard. I pulled back my arm and hurled the hammer. It struck the center of the blackboard. The head remained stuck. The light handle projected from the black surface. All of a sudden I felt tired and disgusted. On the stairs, I found half a mirror. I looked in it. Then I ran home.

Mother was already waiting for me. She looked at me, but said nothing. I didn't tell her where I had been.

Mother served the soup. I began to eat.

At that moment, we heard yells outside our house.

The front door was pushed open, accompanied by shouts.

Herr Resch complained loudly.

Noisily many people clattered up the stairs, past our door and higher.

The Schneiders' door burst open with a bang.

"What's that?" Mother asked, pale and horrified.

We heard a cry—Frau Schneider!

"We must call the police!"

FRIEDRICH

Something fell to the floor with a muffled sound.

"The police don't do anything," I replied. "They watch."

A man's voice swore.

Friedrich cried out, then howled hopelessly.

I threw down my spoon and ran to the door.

"Stay here!" Mother wailed.

I raced up the stairs.

The Schneiders' door dangled from a hinge. The glass had splintered from its frame.

In the kitchen Frau Schneider lay on the floor, her lips blue, her breathing labored.

Friedrich had a lump the size of a fist on his forehead. He bent over his mother, talking to her in a whisper. He didn't notice me.

A man stepped across Frau Schneider's legs without looking down. He emptied a large box of silver cutlery out of the window.

In the living room a woman was smashing china plates. "Meissen!" she said proudly, when she noticed me.

Another woman was slashing every picture in the room with Herr Schneider's letter opener.

A dark-haired giant stood by Herr Schneider's bookcase. He took one volume after another from the shelves. He gripped each book by its binding and tore it apart in the middle. "Bet you can't do the same!" he boasted with a laugh.

In Friedrich's room a man was trying to push the whole bedframe through the window. "Come and help!" he invited me.

I slunk downstairs again.

Mother was peering through a crack in the door, trembling. Fearfully, she pulled me into the apartment. She pushed me into our living room.

We stood by the window and looked down on the street. Above us the crashing and tramping continued.

"Jew, kick the bucket!" a woman screeched outside. It was our newspaper lady.

An armchair rushed past our window and thudded into the rosebushes in our front garden.

Mother began to weep loudly.

I wept with her.

The Death
(1938)

Mother sat up in alarm; I woke up, too. "You, listen!" she said to Father, waking him up.

Father yawned sleepily. "What's the matter, then?" he asked.

"Someone knocked on our door," Mother said.

"You must have dreamed it," Father assured her, and turned on his other side.

"No, I'm sure I didn't," Mother insisted. "I heard it quite clearly."

Before Father could reply, there was another hesitant knock on our apartment door.

Father leaped out of bed immediately. "Well, I never. What time is it?"

Mother looked at the alarm clock. "Half past one," she told him.

Father slid his feet into his slippers. He threw on a coat and shuffled to the door. Without turning on the light, he opened the door a crack.

In the dark outside stood Herr Schneider. He was fully dressed. "Forgive me," he whispered, "but my wife is in a very bad way. We have no lamps and the candle we have gives too weak a light. Could you kindly lend us a table lamp?"

Father opened the door all the way. "But of course, Herr Schneider," he assured him. He got the table lamp from our living room and handed it to him.

Herr Schneider thanked him, adding, "I am very sorry to have disturbed you during the night."

Father shook his head. "Quite all right!" he murmured, softly closed the door, and went back to bed.

"Such excitement!" I heard Mother mutter to herself. "I wonder if I should go and see how Frau Schneider is?" But then she went back to sleep.

I had only just fallen asleep again when there was another knock on our door.

This time Father let Herr Schneider into the apartment right away.

Herr Schneider was accompanied by another man.

"This is Dr. Levy," he told Father. "We have a favor to ask you."

The doctor continued, "I must give Frau Schneider an injection. I found this syringe only this afternoon, retrieved it from the dirt outside, and I haven't been able to boil and sterilize it yet. The Schneiders no longer have a stove."

Mother quickly put on a dress.

I, too, got dressed.

In the kitchen Mother placed the old glass syringe in a large cooking pot.

The doctor smiled in embarrassment. He pointed to the syringe. "The only one I've left." When he saw that the water had still not come to a boil, he asked, "Perhaps I might go ahead to my patient."

Mother nodded. When the water came to a rolling boil, she lifted the pot off the stove. "Take the electric heater upstairs," she told me, carrying the pot up to the Schneiders.

I followed with the electric heater.

The Schneiders' smashed door now leaned against the wall, so one could enter their apartment without hindrance. Inside it was almost pitch dark. One had to feel one's way. Only from the bedroom came a faint shimmer of light.

Because all the doors were gone, Mother cleared her throat loudly. Herr Schneider came and led us to the bedroom.

There everything was utter confusion. The splintered

parts of the bedframe had been piled on top of the wardrobe. The wardrobe no longer had any doors. But they were unnecessary because it no longer contained anything. There was nothing but ruins in the room. The Schneiders had swept the cleared floor space. In the middle, bedded on a pallet of rags, shredded curtains and torn blankets, without any bed linen, lay Frau Schneider. Our table lamp stood on the floor beside her. It threw a warm light on the pained face.

"But you can't leave her like that!" Mother burst out in a horrified voice. "Come on, Herr Schneider, let's carry your wife down to our apartment."

"Too late for that!" murmured Dr. Levy, preparing the syringe.

Herr Schneider stood in the shadows. One couldn't make out his face.

Friedrich was kneeling beside his mother, giving her something from a broken cup.

The wind blowing in through the broken windows fluttered the slashed canvas of a picture. Mother motioned to me to plug in the electric heater. The only plug I could find was already taken up by the table lamp. While Frau Schneider received her injection, I went downstairs to get an extention plug.

When I came back to the bedroom, Frau Schneider was still conscious.

"Confess your sins to your husband," Dr. Levy advised her. He looked directly at Herr Schneider, then moved away.

"Listen, unburden yourself!" Herr Schneider implored her.

Frau Schneider nodded faintly.

The doctor led Friedrich and me out of the room. Mother came with us.

The last thing I saw was Herr Schneider bending over his wife.

"Doctor! Friedrich!" he called out almost at once.

The doctor and Friedrich hurried to the bedroom.

Mother and I followed slowly.

From the doorway I looked into the room. Dr. Levy was lying on his stomach beside Frau Schneider. Very slowly he rose and looked for his hat. He put it on.

Frau Schneider's face had turned quite dark. Her breath came in short bursts. She reared up. Her head flew from side to side. She groaned. Her hands clawed at her chest.

In a strange, chanting voice Dr. Levy began to pray. "Hear O Israel, the Lord our God, the Lord is One!"

Mother folded her hands in prayer. Herr Schneider and Friedrich covered their heads. Then they joined the chant:

> "May the glory of God be eternally praised,
> Hallowed and extolled, lauded and exalted,
> Honored and revered, adored and worshipped."

In the end, Herr Schneider prayed alone, in a hopeless voice: "The Lord, He is God. The Lord, He is God."

And again and again, growing fainter, becoming a murmur, "The Lord, He is God . . ."

Frau Schneider lay still again.

Dr. Levy bent over her. When he straightened up, he shrugged his shoulders. Together with Herr Schneider and Friedrich, he sang, "Praised be you, O Lord God of Truth!"

At that moment Herr Schneider fell on his knees before his wife. With both hands he gripped his shirt collar and tore the shirt. Sobbing loudly, he collapsed.

Friedrich also tore his shirt to shreds. Weeping, he threw himself on his mother's body.

Dr. Levy took a candle from his bag, lit it, and placed it beside the dead woman.

Lamps

(1939)

Herr Schneider had had his broken apartment door mended. He had had to pay for everything himself, even for the ruined rosebushes in Herr Resch's front garden that had suffered from having drawers emptied on top of them.

I rang the bell.

Shuffling footsteps came closer. Herr Schneider peered out at me through a crack. When he recognized me, he listened a moment, opened the door, and pulled me inside.

(100)

He didn't say hello until he had locked the door again.

"I only wanted to deliver this letter which got mixed in with ours by mistake," I said.

Herr Schneider nodded. His hands trembled as he took the letter from me. The hands were dirty. Herr Schneider saw me looking at them and rubbed them on the flowered apron he wore. His "thank you" was barely audible.

We stood in the hall, vacillating. Herr Schneider looked at his letter but didn't open it. I wanted to leave.

"Is Friedrich not at home?" I enquired.

"He's working," answered Herr Schneider, and pointed to the kitchen. With tired steps he led the way and pushed me inside; he still carried the letter in his hand.

The kitchen looked like a lamp shop. Lamps lay, stood, hung, everywhere—the dirty, bent, broken ones to one side and the shining, straight ones that looked like new on the other.

In their midst sat Friedrich. Before him on the kitchen table, handy and in orderly fashion, were arranged rolls of wire, glue pot, paint, cleaning stuff, bulbs of different voltage. He had stuck several screwdrivers, pliers, and knives into the front pocket of his apron.

"What are you doing?" I asked stupidly.

"Mending lamps as you can see!" Friedrich smiled.

Herr Schneider sat down at the table and with a polishing cloth began to clean one of the rusted lamps. While I talked to Friedrich, he sat bent on his stool and didn't once look up from his work.

"Since my father isn't allowed to work any more,"

Friedrich explained, "I just have to provide for both of us. Father collects old lamps from friends and we mend them."

I still looked around me in amazement.

In a few movements Friedrich took apart a standing lamp. Expertly he tested the cable, examined the connection, tightened a little screw, put everything back together again, screwed in a new bulb, tested the lamp by switching it on, nodded contentedly, and set it aside. He handed a wall lamp he'd just cleaned back to his father. "This must be polished some more!" he said pleasantly.

"Our customers expect good work," he explained, turning to me. "If someone isn't satisfied, he won't recommend us. And the more lamps we get, the better off we are." After a pause, he asked: "Don't you know anyone we could do work for? We work cheaply."

"I'll ask around," I promised.

I didn't like it in the cold kitchen. It was so empty. Herr Schneider and Friedrich also seemed different. I didn't know this Friedrich at all. I was leaving when I stepped on the letter. It was still unopened.

"Herr Schneider, your letter," I reminded him and handed it to him.

"Give it to me!" Friedrich demanded.

And since Herr Schneider didn't reach for the letter, I let Friedrich take it.

He tore open the envelope. With dirty fingers he pulled out the letter and read it. Suddenly, his face changed.

With eyes large and helpless, he stared at his father. He sounded desperate when he said, "Herr Resch has given us notice."

Herr Schneider stood up. He pulled Friedrich's head toward him and stroked his hair. "It's hard, boy," he consoled, "but don't worry. He can't do it until he can prove he has another apartment for us to move into."

The fourteen-year-old Friedrich sat at the kitchen table and cried like a small child.

Herr Schneider took me by the shoulder and accompanied me to the door. He shook my hand.

I was already on the stairs when Herr Schneider crept after me. "Visit us again soon!" he whispered. And then, in an even softer voice, he pleaded: "Don't give us away; otherwise, they'll take even the little we have left."

The Movie
(1940)

JUD SÜSS (Sweet Jew) it said in enormous letters over the entrance. At both sides, paintings depicted heads of Jews with beards and earlocks. The movie was in its eighth week. Whole school classes and police divisions marched to it in unison. Everyone was supposed to have seen it.

FRIEDRICH

Because the war restricted most other entertainment, movies were the most important amusement left. And a film so many people talked and wrote about tempted everybody.

Friedrich was waiting for me outside a small soap store. I had once been reprimanded in the Hitler Youth for consorting with a Jew. Since then, we only met in those places where we were unlikely to meet people we knew.

"I looked at the pictures outside," Friedrich told me. "I'm really glad you're going with me. I'd never have dared it alone."

While Friedrich read the reviews exhibited in the showcases, I went to the ticket window. Beneath the price list was an illuminated sign that read:

NO ONE UNDER 14 ALLOWED.

Sometimes they made you show your ID at the ticket window. But no one asked for it this time. And that's what Friedrich had been so afraid of. Although we were already fifteen, Friedrich only had a Jewish identification card.

"Did you get them?" he asked in a whisper, peering around.

I nodded, pleased. Both tickets in hand, I sauntered slowly toward the entrance, looking very confident I was sure.

Friedrich followed behind me, making certain I was always blocking him from the view of the lady examining tickets.

(104)

But she didn't ask for identification either. She didn't even look at us. In a monotone she murmured her, "To your left, please," and let us go inside.

Inside the foyer, Friedrich heaved a loud sigh of relief. "I really don't like this stupid cheating. But a movie like this is really important for me, isn't it?"

We stepped into the dim theater. An usherette received us and led us to our row.

Friedrich thanked her politely.

The usherette smiled kindly.

We were early so we got good seats in the center of the row facing the curtain. Only a few moviegoers sat in the other seats as yet.

But, nevertheless, Friedrich looked in all directions before sitting down on his folding chair. Then he stretched out his legs and enjoyed the comfortable seat. "Up-holstered." he said with pleasure, and stroked the soft armrest.

Meanwhile, a new and older usherette had come in. She took over our side of the cinema, and the younger usherette went over to the other side. She went through our row of seats.

Friedrich jumped up to let her pass.

Again she smiled, gratefully this time.

"Today is the first time since Mother died that I am seeing a movie," Friedrich said softly. "And what a movie! I'm glad Mother didn't have to live through all that's happened in the last two years. We are suffering, and not just because there's a war on."

(105)

FRIEDRICH

Gradually the theater filled up. Seats were taken to the right and left of us. Many young people came to this afternoon performance. The usherettes closed the doors. Everyone waited for the lights to go out.

Suddenly the big ceiling lights went on. Over the loudspeaker a voice announced: "We ask all teenagers to have their ID's ready."

The two usherettes began to go through the rows, starting from opposite ends of the cinema. They glanced briefly at each identification card, sending two or three teenagers out of the cinema. Everything went speedily and quietly.

Friedrich had grown pale. Restlessly, he slid back and forth in his seat. He'd watch the usherettes, and then his eyes would peer along our row.

"What are you getting so nervous about?" I asked, trying to calm him down. "They're only checking to see if we're really fourteen. Just let me handle it; all you have to do is show your ID."

But Friedrich behaved more and more noticeably.

Every one around us turned to stare.

It embarrassed me.

Finally Friedrich bent close to me. Like a little girl he whispered in my ear. "I kept something from you. We Jews aren't allowed to see movies any more. It's forbidden. If they find me here, I'll be sent to a camp. I must get away. Help me, quick!"

The older usherette was pushing her way through to us.

Friedrich still hesitated.

The Movie

The usherette came closer.

Friedrich leaped up.

"Stop!" cried the usherette.

Friedrich tried to squeeze through.

The legs of the other people in our row were in the way.

The usherette caught up with him. "I know what you're up to!" she said loudly, addressing the whole room. "When ID's are examined you disappear and hide, and as soon as it gets dark, you slink back!"

I went and stood beside Friedrich.

"Come on, out with it!" the usherette asked Friedrich. "Then you can go wherever you wish."

"Here it is!" I said, handing her mine.

"I wasn't speaking to you," the usherette said. "It's this one I'm talking to."

"We belong together!" I burst out, but regretted the words the moment I spoke them.

The usherette hadn't been listening.

Friedrich was trembling. His face a dark red, he stammered: "I . . . I . . . I left it at home."

The young usherette had come up from behind. "Why don't you leave the boy in peace!" she suggested. "Don't make such a fuss! It's time anyway!"

Friedrich pleaded: "Please, I want to leave. I'll go voluntarily."

Grinning, the older usherette put her hands on her hips and said, "There's something wrong here, I can tell."

"No, no!" Friedrich protested.

FRIEDRICH

Quick as a flash the usherette grabbed hold of Friedrich's jacket lapels. She put her hand in his pocket. "And what's this here?" she sneered, pulling out the case with Friedrich's ID.

"Give that to me!" Friedrich screamed. "I want my I.D.!" He tried to tear it out of her hand.

But she just leaned back, grinning, holding the case out of his reach.

Friedrich behaved like someone gone mad.

The younger usherette tried to calm him down.

Meanwhile, her colleague was examining Friedrich's identification card. At once, her face grew serious. Without hesitating, she handed the identification back to him. "Come on!" she ordered.

Friedrich pushed through the row and followed her to the side exit. I stayed behind him.

Everyone's eyes followed us.

By the side exit, the usherette took Friedrich's arm and led him outside. Reproachfully, she said, "You must be tired of life! You must be dying to go to a concentration camp, eh!"

Behind us, the lights went out and the victory fanfares of the weekly newscast sounded.

Benches
(1940)

Friedrich suddenly appeared in the center of town. "Can you spare me some time? I want to tell you something. My father wouldn't understand, and anyway, he never listens properly any more. And I have to tell someone, I just have to. Honestly, it won't take long!" Without waiting for my answer, he began to walk beside me.

"It started about four weeks ago," he began. "I was going to collect a pound of noodles which a friend in the suburb had promised us.

"I walked past the old church and through the street with trees—you know, the one where the tram turns left. The trees are all lime trees and they smelled so strongly because they were in bloom then.

"I had gotten as far as the red brick building. I hadn't been paying attention—just meandering along. That's when I suddenly saw the girl in front of me.

"She had very small feet and black hair. I walked behind her for a long time, closely watching how she set down her feet, moved her head, and how she carried the heavy shopping net.

"There were apples in the net, those with the crinkly

skin. How I would have loved one of those apples. 'If one falls out of the net,' I thought, 'I'll speed it away.' I was still picturing this in my mind when the net went 'crack' and all the apples rolled into the street.

"The girl turned at once, put her hands to her mouth, and said: 'What a stinking war-net!' She had gray eyes, gray with a bit of blue in them. They looked great with her black hair. She was just beautiful.

"I helped her pick up the apples. We put them back into the net. But the net wouldn't mend properly, so we carried it together to her house.

"Her name's Helga. Her father is a soldier. She works in a kindergarten. That day, her day off, she had gone to the country and traded hand-knitted potholders for the apples.

"When we got to her door, she looked at me very sweetly and said, 'Thank you. *Auf Wiedersehen!*' She gave me one of the apples as a present. I didn't eat it though. I'm still saving it—as a memory.

"I quickly ran to our friend and picked up the noodles. On my way home, I walked by the kindergarten and asked when she stopped work at night.

"From then on I stood and waited by the kindergarten every evening. As soon as Helga came out, I'd always walk where she had to see me. And when she'd look at me, I always said hello right away.

"At first, her eyes just grew large. She looked even more beautiful then! The third evening, she began to smile when she saw me. At night I dreamed only of Helga.

"A week later she allowed me to walk her home. I can't tell you how happy that made me! We never said much to each other. It was good just walking side by side. Sometimes Helga even looked at me.

"All Helga knew about me was that my name was Friedrich Schneider, nothing else. And I couldn't tell her anything, otherwise she wouldn't have let me meet her any more.

"Well, the Sunday before last we had our first date; we were going to meet in the town park. My father had already wondered what I was doing out every evening. But when he saw me getting dressed up, he shook his head and said: 'Think about what you are doing, Friedrich!' That's all he said; he turned away then. But I went all the same.

"The weather was beautiful. The roses were beginning to bloom. The park was fairly empty. Only a few mothers were pushing their baby carriages around.

"Helga wore a dark-red dress—with her black hair and those gray eyes. When she looked at me, I could feel it inside me. And those small feet! When I think of it!—

"I had brought Helga a slim volume of poetry. And she was so delighted with it that I felt ashamed.

"We walked through the town park and Helga recited poems. She knew many by heart.

"Again and again I searched out lonely paths, where we would hopefully meet nobody. After we had been walking for a while, Helga wanted to sit down.

"I didn't know what to do. I couldn't really refuse her

such a thing. Before I could think of an excuse, we came to one of the green benches and Helga simply sat down.

"I stood in front of the bench, shifting from one foot to the other. I didn't dare sit down. I kept looking to see if anyone was coming.

" 'Why don't you sit down?' Helga asked. But I couldn't think of an answer, so when she said, 'Sit down!' I actually sat down.

"But I wasn't comfortable. What if an acquaintance came by? I slid back and forth on the bench.

"Helga noticed. She took a small bar of chocolate from her pocketbook and gave me some. I hadn't eaten chocolate for who knows how long, but I couldn't enjoy it; I was much too nervous. I even forgot to say thank you.

"Helga had the little book of poems on her lap. She wasn't reading it; she was looking at me. From time to time she'd ask me something. I can't remember what I replied, because I was so terribly afraid, there on that green bench.

"All at once Helga stood up. She took my arm and pulled me along. We hadn't gone far when we reached a yellow bench, which was marked:

FOR JEWS ONLY.

"Helga stopped by this bench and said: 'Would it make you feel better if we sat here?'

"I got a shock. 'How do you know?' I asked.

"Helga sat down on the yellow bench and said, 'It occurred to me.' She said that so simply and matter-of-factly!

"But I really couldn't sit on a yellow bench with this girl. I pulled Helga up and took her home. I could have howled with disappointment. The beautiful Sunday gone! But I was much too nervous to go on walking hand in hand and tell her about me.

"But Helga behaved the whole time as if it were natural to go out with a Jew. She told me about her home, about the children in the kindergarten, and about her vacations. And she took my hand and held it tightly. I could have fallen around her neck and wept! But I was much too excited and stupid to do or say anything sensible like that.

"Helga stopped outside her door. She looked long into my eyes. Then she said: 'We'll meet again next Sunday. But we won't go to the town park. Instead we'll go to the country where there are real woods, where they don't have yellow benches!'

"I tried to talk her out of it, but she stopped me with a kiss and was gone into the house.

"I wandered around town all that evening and half the night. I didn't get home until long after curfew. Luckily no one caught me. But Father was quite furious.

"I debated the whole week whether or not to go. When Sunday came I didn't go after all. I couldn't, you see. The girl would be sent to a concentration camp if she were seen with me!"

The Rabbi

(1941)

An aunt had given us a small sack of potatoes.

That evening I helped Mother put the treasure away and ration it. A little basket was filled for the Schneiders. Mother listened intently. When she heard footsteps above, she sent me upstairs with the basket.

I climbed the stairs, rang the bell and waited. When no one appeared at the door, I rang again.

But nothing moved inside the Schneiders' apartment.

"I could have sworn someone was upstairs!" Mother said. "You can try again when we hear someone go up. Perhaps they just don't want to be disturbed."

A little later Friedrich came up the stairs. I knew his step. I grabbed the basket and tried to catch him on the stairs, but the door fell shut before I could reach him.

Again I pressed the bell, again in vain. After the third ring I put down the basket and knocked because I knew there was somebody in the apartment. "Friedrich!" I called. "Friedrich!"

At last the door opened. But Herr Schneider, not Friedrich, stood before me. He looked at me crossly, then pulled me inside so quickly that I left my basket outside the door.

I had to go out again to fetch the potatoes. Back in the hall I said, "That's why I came, to deliver these potatoes."

Herr Schneider still looked unfriendly. "And you made such a noise just for that?"

"I rang at least ten times," I defended myself, "and no one came to the door even though I could hear someone in the apartment. So I knocked."

Now Friedrich appeared as well. He nodded and took the basket from me. "Why do you scold him?" he asked his father. "Be glad and grateful that he brings us potatoes. You know how much we need them."

Herr Schneider turned away from me. "That still doesn't give you the right to speak to me in that tone of voice!" he spit at his son. "How dare you!"

But Friedrich didn't keep quiet. "Is it my fault that you lose your reason the moment something is demanded of you?"

Herr Schneider's voice grew louder. "It's not me who's lost his reason, but you! Otherwise you wouldn't talk to your own father like that!"

"If you were in your right mind you wouldn't shout!" Friedrich retorted. "Why don't you stand by the window while you're at it, and tell the whole street why you are so upset!"

Beside himself and almost in tears, Herr Schneider answered: "Yes, I'm upset, but I can't help it. I'm afraid. I'm dying of fear!"

"Would you like to throw him out into the street then?" Friedrich hissed. "Do you want to sacrifice him to calm your fears? Ugh!"

His father wept. Sobs shook his body.

Furious and sad at the same time, Friedrich stared at him.

They had apparently forgotten all about me.

Then the living room door opened softly. An old, bearded man stepped out. When he saw me standing in the hall, he was startled. But he controlled himself at once. Calmly, he said: "No one shall quarrel because of me, no one shall be afraid for my sake. I am leaving."

"No!" Friedrich and his father shouted almost simultaneously.

Herr Schneider spread his arms wide and barred the apartment door. His face was wet with tears, but he said: "No, Rabbi, you stay!"

Almost imperceptibly, the rabbi shook his head. "It's too late now. He has seen me!" and he pointed at me.

Friedrich leaped to my side. "I can vouch for him!" he said. "He won't give anything away."

But the rabbi wasn't convinced. "We have too many witnesses and that is bad. Why should I endanger them all? I am old, I will know how to bear it. And the King of the Universe, His name be praised, will help me."

Herr Schneider had regained his control. He pushed the rabbi, Friedrich and me into the living room. Only then did he speak. "This gentleman is a well-known rabbi," he told me.

The rabbi waved this aside and continued, "The Nazis are searching for me. I am hiding in the Schneiders' apartment. Not for long! Friends are going to help me further." He stood right in front of me. "You know what will happen to me if I'm caught? If the Lord our God has pity on me, death—otherwise unspeakable suffering! But this not only threatens me. It also threatens those who have given me shelter and kept me hidden."

I looked at my feet and said nothing.

"I also know," the rabbi continued, "what will happen to you if you don't inform against me. You, and you alone, must decide our fate. If it's too difficult a burden for you to carry, say so, so that we may at least save Friedrich and his father. I will not curse you if you tell me to leave."

Herr Schneider, the rabbi, and Friedrich all looked at me. I didn't know what to do. The rabbi was a stranger to me. And what about my mother and father? Didn't they stand closer to me than this Jew? Might I endanger myself and them for the sake of a stranger? Would I never give myself away? Would I be able to bear the secret or would I suffer under it like Herr Schneider?

The longer I hesitated, the more urgent the three faces before me became.

"I don't know what to do!" I said very softly. "I don't know."

Stars

(1941)

It was quite dark on the stairs. Softly, I knocked the arranged signal: once—long pause—twice—short pause—three times.

Inside I heard cautious noises. Someone opened the door. It stayed dark. A hand slid along the door frame; the lock cracked; a small black gap between frame and door slowly grew wider.

The door only opened all the way after I had whispered my name three times. I slipped inside and waited in the pitch-dark hall until the door had been closed again, equally gently.

A hand touched my arm, held it and pulled me along. I recognized the grip; it was the rabbi.

We crept to the living room.

The rabbi scratched at the door. Then he pushed it open.

There was no light in the living room, either. The rabbi lit a single candle only after we stood inside the room.

The living room had a grim, hopeless look. Every window was thickly covered. By the light spots on the walls one could still make out where the furniture had stood.

On the floor lay a pallet of old blankets, mattresses, and rags. The table in the center of the room seemed the only usable piece of furniture left. And on the table, in all its splendor, sat the candle in its silver Sabbath holder.

"Where is Friedrich?" I asked.

Sitting at the table, Herr Schneider shrugged his shoulders. "Gone to see friends!" he answered. "Curfew must have surprised him there. He'll probably stay there till morning."

The rabbi had sat down. He picked up an old coat from the floor. "You have better eyes than I. Could you please thread this needle for me?" He handed me a needle and a piece of black thread.

While I tried to thread the needle, the rabbi explained: "It's time again, you see. Once more we must wear a yellow star." He pointed to a pile of yellow stars on the table.

The yellow stars with black rims, the size of saucers, had to be fastened over the left breast. They were formed like stars of David. The word "Jew" was woven in the center, in letters resembling Hebrew.

Herr Schneider got up. He bowed to me as if on a stage. Then he undid the knot of his scarf and hung it over the chair. With his left hand he pointed to his left side. On his coat was a yellow star!

He unbuttoned his coat. On his jacket was a yellow star! He opened his jacket. On his waistcoat a yellow star! "In the old days Jews had to wear pointed yellow hats!" His voice was mocking. "This time it's yellow stars—we've gone back to the Middle Ages!"

"And soon," the rabbi added, "soon they'll perhaps burn us, as in the Middle Ages!"

"But why?" I asked.

"Why?" the rabbi repeated softly. "Why? It's decided in heaven who gets raised and who gets humbled. The Lord our God, His Name be praised, has chosen us among all peoples. Because we are different, just because we are different, we are persecuted and killed."

Herr Schneider had sat down again. He pointed to a box where Friedrich usually sat.

Calmly the rabbi stroked the star he had just sewed onto his coat. He put aside the needle and took off his glasses. Looking over the smoky flame of the candle, he began to tell a story:

Solomon

"There once was a king whose advisers came to him and said: 'Lord our Master! Your warriors have long been idle. Payment is poor, and they have been unable to gather booty in either war or revolt. They sit in idleness and think unlawful thoughts. Show them, oh Master, an enemy so that they will not afflict their own people.'

"The king weighed their words carefully, then he commanded: 'If my warriors are in such sore need of deeds, permit them to kill all the Jews in a town you may name. They may keep a third of their booty, but the rest belongs to me, their King.'

"In the town that was selected there lived three devout Jews. The man's name was Schloime, his wife was Gittel, and they had named their son Solomon.

"Schloime heard about the command of their King,

so he went to his wife and said, 'We are both old, what use would it be to flee? We won't get far before we are caught and put to death. Even if we managed to escape, hardship and poverty would follow us. Let us, therefore, sell all that we own. Solomon, our son, shall go; what we receive from the sale of our goods will be sufficient for him to get away. Another land will offer him shelter, and the peace of our Lord will be with him.'

"Gittel, his wife, lowered her head and said meekly, 'Do what you feel is right, the Lord our God is almighty, and no one has explored all His ways.'

"And Schloime sold everything they owned, even their bedstead.

"But before Solomon could make his farewells, the warriors of the king approached their town. Fear and horror preceded them.

"Noise filled the town.

"Kneeling Jews begged for mercy.

"But the warriors' lust for booty made them forget all pity. They entered the town and butchered everything that lived. Ravishing the dead, they entered their houses. They took everything that seemed of value: the goblets made of silver, the cow from its shed. But they destroyed or burned everything they considered useless or worthless.

"When Schloime heard the warriors approaching, he and Gittel hid their son, who knew nothing of the plan his parents had made. Then the two went to meet the warriors.

"Greedily, the warriors searched for treasure. Under threat, they forced Schloime to show them his rooms.

"He willingly led them from cellar to attic; he showed

everything except the hiding place. 'My wife and I, we are old and have lost everything,' he explained.

"The warriors searched the empty rooms in vain and felt Schloime had made fools of them. In their anger, they struck down Schloime and stabbed Gittel, his wife, in the stomach. Then they hurried on, afraid to miss out on booty elsewhere.

"Bleeding, Schloime pulled the screaming Gittel to the door. 'Here,' he said, 'we will die and thus protect Solomon even in death.'

"Gittel nodded. Covering her face with bleeding hands, already dying, she began to pray: 'The Lord is almighty, and His patience is everlasting!'

"Schloime, too, felt his life dwindling from him. He lay down beside his wife and thus barred the entrance against the plundering warriors.

"And while his blood flowed from him in streams, Schloime prayed to his God in tears:

'My God, my God, why hast Thou forsaken me,
And art far from my help at the words of my cry?
O my God, I call by day, but Thou answerest not;
And at night, and there is no surcease for me.
Yet Thou art holy,
O Thou that art enthroned upon the praises
     of Israel.
In Thee did our fathers trust;
They trusted, and Thou didst deliver them.
Unto Thee they cried, and escaped;
In Thee did they trust, and were not ashamed.
But I am a worm, and no man . . .'

"And Schloime died in the middle of his prayer. His blood mingled with Gittel's.

"During their search for booty, the warriors of the king spit on the dead. But they did not cross the bloody barrier. Solomon remained hidden from their eyes because his parents still protected him, even in death.

"Horror and death roamed the town for two whole days. Only smoking ruins and piles of bodies rimmed the paths made by the warriors.

"And Solomon wet the earth with his tears, but still he did not know of his parents' sacrifice, of how they had given their lives to save his. Sadly, he prepared their graves with bare hands. And in the custom of the Holy Scriptures, he honored his parents for seven days, huddling on the earth with naked feet. Then he journeyed to a distant land to seek peace there.

"In their camp, the king's warriors hoped soon to receive new orders that would permit them to lay waste another town."

A Visit

(1941)

We were already in bed when we heard the noise downstairs.

Several men were climbing the stairs to the third floor.

They rang the bell. When no one opened the door, they pummeled it with their fists, shouting: "Open up at once! Police!"

Nothing moved in the Schneiders' apartment.

Father and Mother threw on coats and went as far as our hall. Trembling, we listened behind our door.

"Just a moment, please!" we heard Herr Resch say downstairs. "Don't break down the door! I have a second key! I'll open it for you!" Gasping for air, he dragged himself upstairs.

"That pig!" said my father.

Upstairs we heard the door being unlocked. With a crash it flew against the wall. "Hands up!" shouted a voice.

Then it grew still again. Only heavy footsteps sounded above our heads.

"Let's go outside," Father ordered. The three of us went and stood on the landing.

Shortly thereafter a man wearing a helmet and a trench coat came down the stairs. "Out of the way! Scram!" he snarled when he saw us.

Father took hold of Mother's and my arms. We stayed where we were.

Then came the rabbi. They had put him in handcuffs. A young man pulled him along, smiling at us. The rabbi looked first at Father, then at me, before lowering his head.

Herr Schneider came last. A small man in jackboots accompanied him, holding onto his handcuffs.

A Visit

When Herr Schneider saw my father he said in a loud voice, "You were right, Herr . . . "

A blow from the fist of the little man cut off the sentence; the little man had hit so hard that Herr Schneider reeled under the impact.

Herr Schneider said no more. Blood ran from his lower lip. Once more he looked at us all, lifted his shoulders in resignation, and let himself be dragged along by the little man.

Upstairs the door was being locked.

"One is missing!" Herr Resch screeched. "You forgot one!"

"Shut your mouth!" ordered a clear voice. It belonged to a slim man who was running down the stairs. He held a red folder in his hand. When he noticed us on the landing, he indicated our door with his thumb and said, "Get lost!"

After they had gone, Herr Resch made his groaning way downstairs, clad only in pajamas. He was smiling and, rubbing his hands gleefully, said to Father: "Finally got rid of that irksome tenant! And they caught a pretty bird on top of it!"

Father turned his back on him; pushing us inside the apartment, he flung the door shut so that its glass panes jingled.

Vultures
(1941)

No one slept that night. Father rolled restlessly from side to side, Mother wept, and I thought about Herr Schneider. Though none of us had to go out in the morning, everyone got up very early.

"We must intercept Friedrich when he gets home!" said Mother. "He mustn't even enter their apartment."

Father agreed. "We must prepare him."

Mother couldn't eat any breakfast.

Father drank only a little coffee.

I had to sit behind our door and watch. Breakfast was brought to me there. While I chewed, I kept listening to the noises on the stairs.

There were lots of them this morning. Doors banged; I heard footsteps. But they weren't Friedrich's. I knew his step.

After I had finished my breakfast I stacked the dishes and carried them to the kitchen.

At that very moment Friedrich raced up the stairs.

"Friedrich!" whispered Mother, her eyes full of horror.

Nervously I looked for a place to put down the dishes, finally pushing them into Mother's hands.

"Run!" she said, out of breath.

I ran up the stairs. Friedrich was nowhere to be seen. The door stood open.

I went inside.

Friedrich was in the living room, barring the door with his legs spread wide. Motionless, he stared at Herr Resch.

Herr Resch was kneeling on the floor; his face, pale with fright, was turned toward him. His right hand was stuck inside the mattress; he held his left hand high to ward off Friedrich. He looked like a stone statue. Only his fingers trembled slightly.

Next to him lay Frau Resch's shopping bag. It was filled with Herr Schneider's books. Two lamps showed above the rim; one of the Schneiders' blankets hid the rest. The silver Sabbath holder could be seen because it wouldn't fit in the bag.

The floor was covered with papers, photos, letters. Someone had obviously searched through them and strewn them around.

One of the Schneiders' chests, filled with household things, stood by the door, ready for collection. Herr Schneider's little tool box lay on top.

There wasn't a sound to be heard.

In the street people were talking.

The stillness in the room was horrible.

A car went by outside.

My heart beat so loudly I thought I'd go mad. I didn't dare move.

The stillness seemed to have lasted forever, when Friedrich spit into Herr Resch's face. "Vulture!" he screamed. "Vulture!"

The spittle ran slowly down the face and over Herr Resch's mouth.

He wiped it off with his sleeve. He began to breathe in gasps. Blood came to his face, turning it red. His whole body began to shake. He grabbed for the Sabbath holder and missed. He reached for it a second time and got hold of it.

Friedrich still stood in the doorway, not moving a muscle.

Herr Resch pushed himself off the floor with difficulty. His breath whistling, he staggered toward Friedrich, the silver candleholder in his raised hand.

Friedrich held his ground.

"Help!" Herr Resch's voice rang through the house. "I'm being attacked. Help!"

Friedrich turned calmly, taking his time. Then he saw me. I tried to signal to him.

"Jew!—Stop him!—Police!" screeched Herr Resch. Friedrich merely nodded, went by me and bounded down the stairs—out of the house—away.

The Picture
(1942)

"That Frau Adamek tramples about like an elephant!" Father commented. "You wouldn't think people could make that much noise!"

Mother didn't look up from her knitting; she just nodded.

So Father took up his newspaper once more. He looked at the clock and said, "They'll be here in an hour." The three small suitcases with our most important things in them stood ready by the door. Our coats lay on a chair.

"Don't you want to lie down for a bit before then?" asked Mother.

"No," Father said. "I'll snooze later in the air-raid shelter."

Everything grew quiet again. All one could hear was the ticking of the clock.

I read my book.

Suddenly I heard a tiny noise outside. I listened, but no one but me seemed to have heard anything.

There it was again, a gentle knocking.

This time Father heard it as well. He looked up from his newspaper.

FRIEDRICH

"Someone knocked on our door," I said.

We held our breath and listened.

And there, it came once more: a faint knock, so faint you could barely hear it.

"But that's Friedrich's signal!" I exclaimed, and jumped up.

"Quiet! Stay where you are!" ordered Father, pushing me back into my chair. "Mother will go."

Mother went, not making a sound. When she returned, Friedrich was with her.

Friedrich had turned up the collar of his coat. His coat was stiff with dirt. Furtively, he came to the table and shook hands with Father and me. His hand wasn't clean either. Anxiously he examined our faces and the room; then he whispered: "I won't stay long."

"First of all, you'll sit down," Father decided.

But Friedrich resisted; he didn't even want to take off his coat. When he finally did, we could see that his jacket and trousers were also encrusted with dirt.

Friedrich jumped every time Mother left the room. Father said nothing. Only his eyes were encouraging Friedrich to talk.

It took a long time before Friedrich finally began to talk, haltingly. "I have a hiding place—but I won't tell you where!" he added at once.

"You don't have to," Father said.

"It's terrible—so lonely. I can only think of how it was —but I've forgotten so much, I can't even remember what Father and Mother really looked like. There's nothing to remember them by. Had to sell the watch. This is all I have left!" and from his jacket pocket he pulled the cap to the fountain pen Herr Neudorf, our teacher, had given him for his thirteenth birthday. His name was still legible on it.

"I no longer have the other part," Friedrich explained. "It may have fallen out of my pocket." Tenderly he stroked the cap. When Mother quietly opened the door, he jumped again.

Mother put a large thick sandwich in front of him. She stood and waited until he bit greedily into it, then she went back to the kitchen.

Friedrich wolfed down the sandwich, forgetting even to say thank you. He concentrated on eating. After he had swallowed the last bite almost without chewing, he picked the crumbs off his plate.

Mother gave him two more sandwiches, which went as quickly as the first.

Only then did Friedrich continue. "I need a picture of Father and Mother," he said. "I only came because I know you have one. You know, the snapshot on the horse. I know you have it. Please, may I have it?"

Father thought.

"It can only be in that large box," Mother said, and walked to the closet. She pulled out the giant chocolate box. Father had given her the chocolates for their tenth wedding anniversary because he'd found work again shortly before. Mother opened the box and the topmost photos slid out.

"I'll look through them quickly," Father said, putting aside one picture after the other.

"And you come with me till they find it!" Mother said to Friedrich. She had run a hot bath for him and put some of my clean clothes in the bathroom. At first Friedrich refused, but then he went after all.

The box contained many hundreds of pictures: photos, picture postcards, birthday cards. Father and I searched together, but we had barely sorted through half when the sirens began to wail.

Looking troubled, Friedrich dashed out of the bathroom. "What shall I do now?" he asked, horrified.

"Get dressed for a start!" said Father. Friedrich obediently buttoned the fresh shirt and combed his hair with shaking hands.

"We'll take him to the shelter with us," Mother said.

"Impossible!" said Father. "Resch'll put us in jail."

"But we can't put him out in the street at a time like this," Mother put in. "Just look at the boy."

"The best thing for him to do is stay right here in the apartment," Father decided. "Nothing'll happen, I'm sure. And he can wait here until the air raid is over. Then we'll look further for the photo."

Friedrich accepted the decision without a word.

"But be sure not to put on any light!" Father reminded him. Then we took our suitcases and went out to the air raid shelter.

Friedrich looked after us fearfully.

Antiaircraft guns already thundered outside. Searchlights swayed across the sky. Planes hummed. Shrapnel spattered.

Suddenly two flares lit up the sky, looking like Christmas trees.

In the Shelter
(1942)

The door to the public air-raid shelter was already locked. Father put down his suitcase and maneuvered the iron bars. When the steel door still wouldn't budge, he hammered on it.

Herr Resch opened the door. He wore a steel helmet and an armband identifying him as the air-raid warden. "About time, too!" he growled.

Father said nothing in reply.

We walked into the shelter, greeting everyone there with "Heil Hitler!"

No one answered.

With eyes shut tight, women and old men sat spread over the room. Some had lain down on the benches. Everyone had his luggage beside him. Two mothers and their small children huddled in a dark corner. The children were whining to themselves. In another corner, two lovers sat closely pressed against each other; the man was a sergeant.

We sat down close to the fresh-air pump—where we always sat. The luggage rested between our feet.

Father leaned against the dank, white wall and closed his eyes.

"You'll never get rid of that cough this way," said Mother.

Father sat up straight. "I can't sleep anyway," he said.

"I believe you," nodded Mother.

Herr Resch as air-raid warden crossed the shelter. "Well, comrade, on leave?" he addressed the sergeant.

Startled, the sergeant shot up and agreed.

"We'll show them up there, eh?" Herr Resch was showing off. "Did you read that we shot down thirty-five enemy bombers yesterday?"

The sergeant smiled. "And thirty-five others are taking their places today, and God knows how many more will come!"

Herr Resch cleared his throat. Without another word, he turned and went back to the door.

The sergeant once more embraced his girl.

Outside the pounding grew louder, and the bark of our antiaircraft guns sounded strangely hollow. The shots mingled with the sounds of bombs exploding, singly first, then several at once. Whole groups of bombs fell together. The cellar resounded with their explosions.

"The poor boy!" sighed Mother.

Father just said, "Hmm."

Herr Resch withdrew to the shelter proper, closing the airlock and making the shelter airtight.

Again a bomb exploded. This time, it hit so close the cellar walls shook under the impact.

Suddenly there came a pounding on the door.

"Who can that be so late?" muttered Herr Resch, searching the room.

"Well, go and open up!" the sergeant called from his corner.

Herr Resch unbarred the inner door. Now we could hear someone whimper outside. "Please, please let me in. Please, pleeease!"

"Friedrich!" Mother burst out. Her mouth fell open, her eyes grew large.

"Open up! Open up!" the voice shouted, full of horror. "Please, open up!"

Herr Resch opened the steel door.

Friedrich was kneeling outside, his hands folded in prayer. "I am afraid. Afraid. Afraid." On all fours, he crept into the airlock of the shelter.

Through the open door we could hear how hellish it was outside. The pressure of another hit threw the steel door shut.

"Out!" bellowed Herr Resch. "Scram! You don't really imagine we'd let you into our shelter, do you?" His breathing was labored. "Out! Get out!"

The sergeant stood up and walked over to Herr Resch. "Have you gone out of your mind? You can't send the boy out of a shelter in this raid!"

(135)

"Do you know who that is?" Herr Resch sputtered. "That's a Jew!"

"So?" the sergeant asked with astonishment. "And even if it were but a dog, you'd let him stay until the raid is over."

The other people in the shelter also took part now. "Let the boy stay!" came from all sides.

"Who do you think you are!" Herr Resch screamed. "How dare you mix in my affairs? Who is air-raid warden here, you or I? You follow my orders, is that understood? Otherwise I'll report you."

No longer sure of himself, the sergeant stood and looked at Friedrich. Everyone was silent. The guns still sounded.

Very pale, Friedrich still leaned in the airlock. He had calmed down.

"Go, boy. Go voluntarily!" the sergeant said softly. "Otherwise there'll be nothing but annoyance."

Without a word Friedrich left the shelter.

Shots and bombs thundered without a break. We could even hear the whistling sound of the falling bombs and the rushing sound of the incendiary bombs.

Mother cried against Father's shoulder.

"Do pull yourself together!" begged Father. "You'll endanger us all otherwise."

The End

(1942)

Dust and heat greeted us outside. The sky glowed red with the light of fires. Flames still came from roofs and hollow windows. Heaps of rubble smoldered. Glass splinters and fragments of tiles covered the street. In-between lay the incendiary bombs that had missed their targets.

Desperate women cried in front of ruins from which clouds of dust and pulverized brick still rose. Beside a garden wall lay a human being. Someone had thrown a shredded slip over the face.

Supporting Mother between us, we searched for the way home.

Herr and Frau Resch came with us.

A bomb had ripped open the street outside our house, but the house still stood. The roof was partly uncovered and none of the windows had any glass.

We stepped into the front garden.

At once Herr Resch made for the little bit of lawn. He picked up his garden dwarf, Polycarp. A piece of shrapnel had cut off the tip of his cap. Herr Resch searched for it. When he discovered it despite the darkness, he said to Father: "What a shame! I'll try to glue it back on."

Fearfully, Mother looked for Friedrich.

Friedrich sat in the shadow of the stoop. His eyes were closed, his face pale.

"Are you crazy?" Father couldn't help asking.

At that Herr Resch also noticed him.

Father was still standing on the path. It was obvious he didn't know what to do.

Herr Resch pushed his wife aside and stepped closer, still carrying Polycarp.

"Away from here!" he thundered at Friedrich. "Do you think you no longer have to fear being sent away, just because everything's out of whack after this raid?"

Shrilly Mother said: "Can't you see he's fainted!"

A mocking smile on his face, Herr Resch turned to Mother and said: "Fainted indeed! I'll get him out of it quickly enough. But I must say I am surprised at your sympathy for a Jew. You, the wife of a member of the Nazi party."

Father pulled her aside. She was sobbing.

Herr Resch lifted his foot and kicked.

Friedrich rolled out of the shelter entrance way onto the stone path. A trail of blood went from his right temple to his collar.

I clutched the thorny rosebush.

"His luck that he died *this* way," said Herr Resch.

Chronology

Dates given for laws, decrees, and regulations are dates of public announcement.

(1933)

January 30, 1933	Adolf Hitler becomes Chancellor of the German Reich. He is the Supreme Leader of the NSDAP (National Socialist German Workers Party) and the S.A. (storm troopers).
March 5, 1933	Adolf Hitler receives a strong vote of confidence from the German people in the *Reichstagswahl* (parliamentary elections).
March 24, 1933	The *Reichstag* (German Parliament) empowers Hitler to enact laws on its behalf.

April 1, 1933	Adolf Hitler proclaims a one-day boycott of all Jewish shops.
April 7, 1933	All non-Aryan civil servants, with the exception of soldiers, are forcibly retired.
April 21, 1933	Kosher butchering is forbidden by law.
April 25, 1933	Fewer non-Aryan children are admitted to German schools and universities.
June 16, 1933	There are 500,000 Jews living in the Third Reich.
July 14, 1933	German nationality can be revoked—for those considered "undesirable" by the government.

(1934)

August 2, 1934	Paul von Hindenburg, second president of the German Republic, dies.
August 3, 1934	Adolf Hitler declares himself both President *and* Chancellor of the Third Reich.

(1935)

March 16, 1935	Compulsory military service is reinstituted in Germany in open defiance of the Versailles Treaty.
September 6, 1935	Jewish newspapers can no longer be sold in the street.
September 15, 1935	*Nürnberg Laws* deprive Jews of German citizenship and reduce them to the status of "subjects"; forbid marriage or any sexual relations between Jews and Aryans; forbid Jews to employ Aryan servants under the age of 35.

(1936)

March 7, 1936	Jews no longer have the right to participate in parliamentary elections.
	The German army reoccupies the Rhineland.
August 1, 1936	The Olympic Games are opened in Berlin. Signs reading "Jews

Not Welcome" are temporarily removed from most public places by order of the Führer—to present a favorable and misleading picture to foreign tourists.

(1937)

July 2, 1937

More Jewish students are removed from German schools and universities.

November 16, 1937

Jews can obtain passports for travel abroad only in special cases.

(1938)

March 11, 1938

German troops march into Austria.

July 6, 1938

Jews may no longer follow certain occupations such as broker, matchmaker, tourist guide.

July 23, 1938	As of January 1, 1939, all Jews must carry identification cards.
July 25, 1938	As of September 30, 1938, Jewish doctors can be regarded only as "medical attendants."
July 27, 1938	All "Jewish" street names are replaced.
August 17, 1938	As of January 1, 1939, all Jews must have only Jewish first names. If a Jew has a German first name, "Israel" or "Sarah" must be added to it.
October 5, 1938	Jewish passports are marked with a "J."
October 28, 1938	About 15,000 "stateless" Jews are "resettled" in Poland.
November 7, 1938	Herschel Grynszpan, a Jew, attempts to assassinate the German Attaché, vom Rath, in Paris.
November 9, 1938	Vom Rath dies. Goebbels, recognizing the propaganda value, issues instructions that "spontaneous demonstrations" against Jews are to be "organized and executed" throughout Germany—in retaliation! The pogrom begins.

November 10, 1938	Pogrom continues.
November 11, 1938	Jews may no longer own or bear arms.
November 12, 1938	Following the Nazi-organized pogrom, "reparations" of one billion *Reichsmarks* are imposed on the German Jews, and they must further repair all damages at their own cost.
	Jews may no longer head businesses.
	Jews may no longer attend plays, movies, concerts, and exhibitions.
November 15, 1938	All Jewish children remaining in German schools are removed to Jewish schools.
November 23, 1938	All Jewish businesses are closed down.
November 28, 1938	Jews may no longer be in certain districts at certain times.
December 3, 1938	Jews must hand in their drivers' licenses and car registrations.
	Jews must sell their businesses and hand over their securities and jewelry.

December 8, 1938	Jews may no longer attend universities.

(1939)

March 15, 1939	German troops march into Czechoslovakia.
April 30, 1939	Rent protection for Jews is reduced.
May 17, 1939	About 215,000 Jews still live in the Third Reich.
September 1, 1939	Germany declares war on Poland.
September 3, 1939	WORLD WAR II begins. (Curfew for Jews is instituted: 9 p.m. in summer, 8 p.m. in winter.)
September 21, 1939	Pogroms against Jews in Poland.
September 23, 1939	All Jews must hand in their radios to the police.
October 12, 1939	Austrian Jews are beginning to be deported to Poland.
October 19, 1939	"Reparations" for German Jews are increased to 1.25 billion *Reichs-*

marks and are now payable by November 15, 1939.

Noverber 23, 1939   Polish Jews must now wear yellow stars of David.

(1940)

February 6, 1940   Unlike the rest of the German people, Jews do not receive clothing coupons.

February 12, 1940   German Jews begin to be taken into "protective custody," that is, deported to concentration camps.

July 29, 1940   Jews may no longer have telephones.

(1941)

June 12, 1941   Jews must designate themselves as "unbelievers."

July 31, 1941   Beginning of the "final solution."

September 1, 1941	Every Jew in Germany must also wear a star of David.
	Jews may no longer leave their places of residence without permission of the police.
October 14, 1941	The large-scale deportation of Jews to concentration camps begins.
December 26, 1941	Jews may no longer use public telephones.

(1942)

January 1, 1942	Approximately 130,000 Jews now live in the Third Reich.
January 10, 1942	Jews must hand in any woolen and fur clothing still in their possession.
February 17, 1942	Jews may no longer subscribe to newspapers or magazines.
March 26, 1942	A Jewish apartment must be identified as such with a star of David beside the name plate.

April 24, 1942	Jews are forbidden the use of public transportation.
May 15, 1942	Jews are forbidden to keep dogs, cats, birds, etc.
May 29, 1942	Jews are no longer permitted to visit barber shops.
June 9, 1942	Jews must hand over all "spare" clothing.
June 11, 1942	Jews no longer receive smoking coupons.
June 19, 1942	Jews must hand over all electrical and optical equipment, as well as typewriters and bicycles.
June 20, 1942	All Jewish schools are closed.
July 17, 1942	Blind or deaf Jews may no longer wear armbands identifying their condition in traffic.
September 18, 1942	Jews can no longer buy meat, eggs, or milk.
October 4, 1942	All Jews still in concentration camps in Germany are to be transferred to (extermination camp) Auschwitz.

(1943)

April 21, 1943   Jews found guilty of crimes are to be conveyed to extermination camps in Auschwitz or Lublin after serving their sentences.

(1944)

September 1, 1944   Approximately 15,000 Jews now live in the Third Reich.

(1945)

May 8, 1945   END OF WORLD WAR II. Collapse of the Third Reich.

ABOUT THE AUTHOR

Hans Peter Richter was born in Cologne, Germany, between the two World Wars. He studied sociology and psychology at the universities of Cologne, Bonn, Mainz, and Tübingen, earning his doctor's degree. He is the author of more than twenty books for children and young adults, in addition to a number of professional publications in his field. His interests in literature, history, and current events have made him a frequent guest on radio and TV shows throughout Europe. Dr. Richter now lives in Mainz, Germany.

ABOUT THE TRANSLATOR

Edite Kroll was born and raised in Germany, and completed her education at Cambridge University in England, and the *Alliance Française* in Paris. Long involved with children's literature, she has worked as an editor of juvenile books both in England and the United States. Now a freelance editor/ translator, Mrs. Kroll lives in North Yarmouth, Maine, with her husband, writer Steven Kroll.

Temple Israel

Minneapolis, Minnesota

In honor of the Bar Mitzvah of
JAMES SANDERS
by
Mr. & Mrs. David Sanders